First published in Great Britain by Amazon

The moral right of the author has been asserted.

All rights reserved. Without limiting the rights under copyright reserved above, no part of this publication may be reproduced, stored or introduced into a retrieval system, or transmitted, in any form or by any means (electronic, mechanical, photocopying, recording or otherwise), without the prior written permission of both the copyright owner and the publisher of this book.

The characters, the events and places in this book are fictious. Any similarity to real persons, dead or alive, event or place is coincidental and not intended by the author.

Copyright © 2024 Krystal Zammit

All rights reserved.

ISBN: 9798302431615

For my dad, these words, this story, belong to no one but you.

CONTENTS

	Acknowledgments	i
1	10-11	1-25
2	21-22	26-63
3	32-33	64-82
4	43-44	83-98
5	54-55	99- 112
6	Timeless	113-122

ACKNOWLEDGMENTS

Four years ago, it was my father who sat me down and told me about this story, igniting the spark that would eventually lead to its creation. None of this would be here without his dedication, belief, and love.

To my mother, who not only supported me but also put up with my father through it all—thank you for your patience and strength.

Lastly, to Ralph, you were here for so many milestones in my life, I wish you could see this one.

CHAPTER 1
10-11

'Get on the bike, Jake.'

Jake must have misheard him. There were many rules his father enforced, but his number one rule was: '*never, under any circumstances, touch the bike.*'

His father's fingers were lined with oil and muck as he circled around the 1951 Vincent Black Lightning. Dark eyes studied the motorbike, before he pointed at it.

'Son, get on the damn bike.'

Jake was so tiny next to the mechanical beast, so his father had to give him a boost up. It felt clumsy as his scrawny legs straddled the bike, leaning forward to touch the handles that were too big for his clammy palms.

'This will be yours one day, Jake. You need to get comfortable with it.'

The cold metal continued to bite into Jake's skin.

'I don't understand.' Jake muttered, wiggling his backside, trying to find a position that didn't make his thighs ache.

From inside the house, his mother's melody drifted through the open window. It started soft, a gentle ripple like the first touch of sunlight on water, before swelling into something richer, fuller - a cascade of sound that filled the air. Jake froze for a moment, the unfamiliar hum of the bike's engine blending with the familiar, comforting tune of the piano. He tilted his head, the music tugging at something deep inside him.

His father's voice was purposeful when he said, 'This is yours, son. Your legacy is this bike.'

From the house, Jake's mother continued her melody.

The air smelt musty and the playground was heaving. They were barely five minutes into their lunch-time and students were already whizzing past Jake, lunchbox in hand, yelling. Some of the bigger boys were demanding to play bulldog, others suggested football. Some girls lingered close to the frantic boys, others stayed by the fence and quietly munched on their sandwiches. Like a puzzle, each student fell rightfully into their place within their group. Jake loitered for a moment. He leant his back on the fence and wrapped his arms around him. Despite his best efforts to curl himself small, Marco, amongst his usual big crowd, spotted Jake across the playground.

'SHAKEY JAKEY!'

Pulling the straps of his bag tight, Jake hurried away. He wasn't going to wait for the boys to decide on a game; he assumed it would be football, and that was good enough for him. Later, when his mother inevitably asked what he did at school, he would tell her that football was exactly what he played. He'd say he tackled someone, they got angry, but overall, it was fun. His mother would smile, and that would be all the reassurance Jake needed to know his little white lie was harmless.

Checking that Marco wasn't on his tail, Jake quickly strode to the music block. It was comfortably quiet, broken only by the sweet harmony of different instruments drifting through the air. The sound emanated from beyond the doors, which were wedged shut: the private rooms. Intermittently, Jake could hear the soft murmur of instructional voices.

'No, no, silly, you need C sharp!'

'Lift your head up, girly, what are you doing? Falling asleep?'

'Come on, don't give up yet!'

Jake did not have a private tutor. His parents could never afford it. Instead, he had Mrs P - the school's music teacher. She was feared by many and loved by few. She laid a strict law in her classroom that many students resented following, especially the likes of Marco and his crew.

Only a few weeks ago, Mrs P threatened to suspend Marco for his unruly behaviour and that's exactly why Jake adored her. And that's why he decided to spend every break and lunch with her, rather than anyone else his age.

'Back again are we, Jacob?' Mrs P said, biting on an apple as he entered her classroom. The grand piano here was a lot nicer than the one at home. It shined bright and looked brand new, but it was missing something important. It didn't have the touch of his mother. 'Have you had a good day today, Jacob?'

He didn't know why she called him Jacob, his name was *Jake*. It said so on his birth certificate, but he never corrected her. Instead, he nodded his head, his finger playing the first three chords of his mother's song.

'The department was given a new instrument today.' The apple now bitten to the core. 'Would you like to see it?'

Surrounded by maracas, trombones, flutes, recorders, and the grand piano resting under his fingertips, Jake couldn't imagine what other treasures she might have hidden away. From beneath her desk, Mrs. P pulled out a black case. It was too small to hold a trombone but too large for a flute. She beckoned him closer and a delicate shiver ran down Jake's spine as she slowly unclipped the case. Light bounced off polished wood, illuminating the violin as Mrs. P revealed it. It was breath-taking.

'Would you like to hold it?'

Jake extended his hands, nodding eagerly, but Mrs. P held it close to her chest, raising a thin eyebrow. She had made it abundantly clear, many times, that a nod was not an acceptable response.

'Yes, please, Mrs. P.'

The instrument was lighter than he thought it would be. The wood was soft and the strings were taut. His chin lowered onto the rest and he exhaled. It felt good.

'That's it,' she encouraged. 'You look like a natural.'

When she finally handed him the bow, Jake held it carefully, the weight both delicate and strange in his hand. He rested it gently on the strings, but as he drew it across, a sharp, jarring sound pierced the air, making him flinch. The violin seemed to protest under his unpractised touch, the note screeching like a stubborn hinge. Mrs. P winced but quickly masked it with a smile.

'Not quite, Jacob,' she said softly. 'Let's try that again, this time, with a bit more control.' Mrs P took the instrument back and asked him to listen. So he did, listening the way he listened to his mother play the piano. The notes from the violin were like no other.

'Wow.' Jakes exhaled.

Mrs P stopped playing and smiled.

'Would you like to learn?'

Yes, he did. There was a part of him that longed to play the violin, perhaps even more than the piano. The thought sparked a guilty pang in his chest, as though he were betraying his mother, who had always been so proud of his piano playing. Yet, the violin called to him in a way the piano never had, its voice raw and emotive, full of possibilities. But none of it mattered. Jake would never step foot inside the private practice rooms where real violinists honed their craft. The cost of that kind of tutoring was a luxury his family couldn't afford. That reality weighed heavy, like the violin now out of his reach.

'I'll teach you, at lunch, Jacob. Under one condition that is.' She knelt down. 'You promise that you create your own song rather than replicate your mother's.'

The piano that loomed behind him, once so commanding and familiar, seemed smaller now. The violin in Mrs P's hands seemed alive, its wooden body glowing. The curves of the instrument caught the light, reflecting warmth and Jake couldn't look away. The piano, his constant companion, now felt like a distant friend.

'Yes Mrs P, I promise.'

She handed him the instrument.

For the rest of the school day, the sweet notes of the violin played delicately in Jake's ears. He had a long way to go before he felt comfortable with the instrument, but Mrs P remained remarkably patient. She guided his fingers from one string to the other, reminding him to loosen his grip and not fear the instrument, but rather lean into it. It was a peculiar expression, but it made sense, his mother often moved with her piano.

During maths, his fingers itched. Algebra did not sound as sweet as the violin, so instead of trying to figure out the formula, Jake wrote down all of the tips and tricks Mrs P taught him during lunch. Thankfully, the bell rang before his teacher had the chance to see Jake's workbook and he darted out of the school and its forsaken gates.

Jake knew better than to leave straight away. He should have hung back, maybe even waited in the restroom until everyone had cleared out. But caught up in the daydream of one day playing the violin for thousands, the imagined applause of a cheering audience quickly dissolved into the jeers and heckling of Marco and his mates.

'SHAKEY JAKEY!'

They probably couldn't see his knees trembling, but it didn't matter, they were right. Just the sound of their voices was enough to make Jake shake. He knew better than to turn around. Eye contact would only escalate things, turning it into a standoff he was certain he'd lose. Thick grey clouds started to hang heavy above Jake's head as he remained light on his feet, weaving between the clusters of children also heading home. The lollipop man at the end of the road didn't seem to notice the fear in his eyes when Jake reached the point of decision: cut through the woods or take the longer route around. The woods were a tempting shortcut, offering a faster escape, but they also meant isolation, like prey wandering into the jaws of a predator.

'Go on, JACOB! Walk through the forest, you pansy!' one of the boys bellowed, his voice deep and menacing. Jake hesitated when a stone struck his bag with a loud thud, bouncing to the ground. Before he could react, a second, heavier stone hit his arm. Pain shot down to his elbow, and instinctively, Jake raised his hands to shield himself before breaking into a desperate run.

He didn't even realise where he was going until he stopped to catch his breath, his chest heaving. The shortcut. The woods. In his panic, Marco and his gang had forced him onto their chosen battlefield. Now it was their turn to chase, their footsteps pounding behind him, Marco's voice barking commands.

Jake tried to leap over a thick bed of weeds, but his foot caught, throwing him off balance. Before he could recover, Marco slammed into him, tackling him to the ground with the force of a rugby player. The impact drove the air from Jake's lungs as they tumbled, dirt and mud smearing their clothes and skin. Jake's heart pounded in his ears, the sting of humiliation as sharp as the ache in his chest. The hollering grew louder as Marco's fists pounded into Jake's body. Jake curled up, shielding his face with his arms, his voice breaking as he yelled for help from the birds in the trees, from the sly fox hidden in its den. But nothing stirred. The forest remained silent, indifferent, as Jake braced himself against each blow, swallowing his cries. Hot tears streaked his cheeks, and no matter how desperately he tried to block Marco's punches, the other boy's strength overwhelmed him.

Then, just as suddenly as it had started, the assault stopped.

A cool breeze brushed against Jake's sweat-dampened skin, filling the space where Marco's fists had been. For a moment, everything was still.

'Get off him!' a voice squealed.

'Jeeez, Annabelle, we're only having a laugh!'

'Doesn't look like no laugh to me!'

Annabelle's voice rang out, fierce and protective. With a sudden tug, she pulled Marco off Jake, her hands strong as she yanked him away. Marco stumbled back, his expression twisted, but he didn't argue. Annabelle stood tall, eyes blazing, squaring up to him as she shouted,

'You're just bullies, the lot of you!'

Meanwhile a pair of watery eyes scanned over Jake's bruised body. 'Are you okay?'

It wasn't Annabelle helping him to sit upright, but her friend Lottie, her gentle hands guiding Jake to his feet. He recognised them both from school. Annabelle, still fuming, kept her focus on Marco.

'We were just-'

'No! No 'justs'!' Annabelle snapped, cutting him off before he could defend himself.

'Damn,' Lottie chuckled, she was picking mud and leaves from Jake's stained clothes. 'You don't wanna' anger Annie, that's for sure.'

Grunting, Marco looked at Jake, his eyes briefly softening as he seemed to register the damage he'd caused. But the moment passed quickly, and his face hardened again. 'You bitch,' he muttered to Annabelle, before instructing his mates to follow as they stalked off.

Lottie sighed, 'They're all like-'

'Monkeys.' Annabelle cut in. 'The lot of 'em.' Her face softened as Jake shakily stood to his feet. 'Are you okay?'

'Yeah, *are* you okay?' Lottie's voice was high-pitched. 'I mean, Annie and I were just walking home when we heard yelling and screaming and then we saw Marco absolutely going-'

'Lottie.' Annabelle pressed. 'Let him speak.'

It took Annabelle asking Jake, yet again, how he was. He ached and it hurt to move, but he managed to nod.

'Do you need some help?'

Jake shook his head, his skull now aching.

'Well, lemme' walk you home.'

'Let *us* walk you home!' Lottie jumped in.

'No, it's okay.' Blood trickled down his lips. 'I'm okay.'

'Well, I insist.' Annabelle smiled.

Unsure if his face was hot from the beating or the butterflies fluttering in his stomach, Jake nodded. Annabelle wore the nicest smile he had ever seen.

'Well, you lead, I follow.'

Trying not to show his ache, Jake started walking and hoped he was not displaying any obvious signs of a limp.

'You're the one who's always in the music block, aren't ya? Jake, right?' Annabelle asked, tilting her head as she looked at him, her tone softening a little.

'Yeah! He is! I see him all the time there. He's always with Mrs P!' Lottie piped up eagerly. Annabelle rolled her eyes when Lottie wasn't looking, mouthing *sorry about her* with a playful, exasperated expression. Jake stifled a laugh, grateful for the brief lightness. A minute or two later, clearly growing bored of the scene, Lottie glanced at her watch and announced she was going to head home.

'I'll catch you tomorrow, though, Jake? In English?' she asked with a smile, as though the exchange hadn't been awkward at all. Jake hadn't even realised Lottie was in his English class, but he nodded, feeling a little surprised at the invitation. He thanked her for helping, even though, deep down, he knew Annabelle had been the one to really step in. With Lottie gone, the silence between Jake and Annabelle grew thicker. It wasn't uncomfortable exactly, but the quiet was charged. They continued to walk until Annabelle broke it with a laugh.

'Wow, you are real quiet, aren't ya?'

'Oh, I'm sorry.'

'Wait,' Annabelle faltered. 'Why are you apologising?'

His whole life, Jake had been told he needed to speak up and stand taller.

'My father… he says I just need to be louder.'

'Funny that,' Annabelle giggled. 'My father always tells me I need to be more quiet.' Her voice travelled between the gaps of the trees. 'How about we make a pact? I don't apologise for bein' loud and you don't apologise for bein' quiet?' They broke out into a clearing of the forest near the main road by Jake's house. The sky was lighter than it had been before the attack, the threat of rain clearing.

'Deal.' Jake finally said. He then pointed across the road, informing Annabelle that's where he lived.

'Well then Jake, this is where our journey ends!' She pulled an elastic band from her wrist and began to pull her long blonde hair into a tight ponytail. 'For today at least!

As she crossed the road, Annabelle called out to him, 'Next time those boys give you grief, punch one of them in the nose, or kick 'em in the gonads! Because if you don't, I will!' Her voice carried, and she laughed as she walked away. Jake knew she wasn't joking, especially with the way she laughed.

'My lord! Jake, what happened to you?' Mother squealed, putting the knife down and neglecting the carrots on the chopping board. There was a heavy ache in his muscles but the attack felt distant. He had completely forgotten that a swollen eye and muddied clothes would worry his mother.

He smiled through his cracked lip, 'I made a friend.'
Before she had the chance to press further, Jake walked out of the kitchen. As he passed the piano, he glided his fingers

across the keys. It made him yearn for the violin.

Dinner was eaten in silence. Mother glanced worriedly at Jake, who took minuscule mouthfuls to avoid splitting his lip open again. It only just stopped bleeding. Jake's father sipped on his whiskey, his food untouched. Jake knew it was bad when Mother sent him to bed without making him clean the dishes.

'Just get on with your homework.'

Jake did not get on with his homework. Instead, he left his bedroom door ajar and leant his ear into the gap. Their conversation started as a whisper, but soon they spoke freely, most likely believing their son's head was buried in a textbook.

'Something is seriously wrong, Frank.'

'What the hell do you want me to do about it?'

'Did you not see your son's face? Someone's beating on him!'

'We all get pushed around at school, Annette, for Christ's sake.'

'Not like that! I have a good mind to go in–'

'No! You leave him be. He needs to learn to defend himself, grow a damn voice.'

'Frank!'

Fists slammed onto a table.

'You listen here, that boy will one day have to learn to stand on his own two feet. We will not be here to coddle him, protect him. He will be alone and not have a damn clue on how to navigate it. So no, you and I will not interfere. Our son will defend himself and grow a god-damn back bone.'

It was the sound of his mother crying that gave Jake the courage to walk back downstairs and poke his head into the dining room.

'Please don't cry. Please don't argue.'

His parents looked at each other, and then away.

'Jakey, it's okay, we were just talking.' His mother said, trying to smile as she tucked a tissue into her sleeve. His father's face was tight. A deep set sadness withered into the wrinkles around his eyes.

'I know what I need to do,' Jake nodded.

'And what would that be, son?' his father asked.

'I'll–' He took a deep breath. 'I'll punch 'em square in the nose and kick them in the gonads if they ever give me grief.'

His mother gasped, but it was replaced by the roaring laughter of his father.

'That's my boy! Come here!'

With open arms, Jake rushed into his father's embrace. Despite the ache in his bones, Jake nestled as close as he could.

'And I'll never be alone, Dad.' Jake muttered into his father's chest. 'Because I made a friend today.'

The black eye looked worse in the morning. It bulged out of his socket, making it difficult for Jake to see properly. His mother tried to hide her grimace, but failed. She did manage to say goodbye without crying, hugging Jake extra tight.

'Have a good day!' She hollered as Jake pulled his backpack strings. 'Be careful!'

As he crossed the road, he squinted at a figure leaning against an oak tree, busy plaiting her long, wet blonde hair. It only took a moment for him to recognise Annabelle's familiar silhouette.

'Finally!' Annabelle yelled, her voice muffled. Two pink clips were held between her teeth. 'Do me a favour?'

It took Jake a moment to realise she was expecting him to take the clips. He hovered his hand near her mouth, and she gently parted her lips, allowing the clips to fall. They were damp.

'Thanks! My mouth was nearly crampin'.' She dropped the plait from her fingers and then pried the clips from Jake's hand, pinning loose hairs back. 'How are you holding up today?'

Jake shrugged. 'I'm okay.' They started walking and when they were halfway through the forest, he added, 'My mother is very worried.'

'I don't blame her. I mean, look at you. You should tell a teacher.'

Jake shook his head so fast it made his eye and lip ache.

'I don't get it. Why not?'

He didn't answer. There was no need, not when they reached the school gates five minutes later and every student turned to gawk at him and his swollen lip. He didn't even make it to period one before he was called to the headmaster's office.

Headmaster Keither pressed him hard, reminding Jake that it was his duty to protect his classmates and stand up to bullies. Jake shrugged, as he often did. It frustrated Keither, as it often did with adults. But Jake made it to break in time and quickly headed toward the music block. He couldn't afford to miss any practice on the violin. Just as he reached the doors, Marco suddenly stepped in front of him. Jake was surprised to see him there, but even more surprised that Marco was alone, with none of his usual gang in sight.

'You alright?' Marco grunted. His hands were tucked tightly in his pockets and his chin dipped to his chest. It was the first time Jake ever saw him with soft eyes. 'I heard Keither called you.'

'Yeah, he did.'

From the window in the music room, Mrs P hovered. She waved at Jake but not long before her thin eyebrows narrowed upon noticing Marco. She wouldn't wait to shoo him away.

'I just wanna' say thank you,' Marco scratched the back of his head, still not looking up. 'You know, for not ratting.'

Mrs. P's voice was far from kind or soft when she told

Marco to bugger off and find someone else to annoy. As he stalked away, he muttered a quiet 'thanks.' It was so soft that Jake wasn't sure he'd actually heard it. The words didn't make sense to him. Marco, kind? Maybe by tomorrow, Marco would be back to his old tormenting ways.

'Welcome back, Jacob.' Mrs P smiled. 'You have a friend waiting for you.'

Jake didn't know who to expect, but there she was, Annabelle, perched at the edge of the piano. Twice now, she had waited for him. Her presence felt like it belonged there, like it had always been this way.

'I-I hope you don't mind,' Annabelle said, standing. She twizzled the edges of her long hair. 'I remember you said you like to-'

'It's fine.' Jake replied, smiling. The violin was on Mrs P's desk, already open. He reached for it. 'Would you like to see me play?'

Marco kept his word. He didn't bother Jake for the rest of the week, nor for the entire term. By the time Jake's eleventh birthday came around, he had actually begun to enjoy school. Sitting together in the music room, Jake couldn't help but ask Annabelle, 'Why?' He didn't understand why she'd choose to spend her free-time in the music room instead of outside with her many other friends. Even Lottie, who never hid her crush on Jake, didn't sacrifice her lunch breaks, using them to braid girls' hair and cheer for the boys in their sports games.

'Why not?' Annabelle replied, her tone casual.

'That's not an answer,' Jake pointed out, a hint of frustration creeping in.

Annabelle rolled her eyes dramatically, as she always did when she felt cornered. 'Well, it's the only one you're getting.'

Before Jake could press for more, Mrs. P came hurdling through the door, her voice cutting through the conversation as she instructed him to pick up the violin and play. He had no time to respond or argue. As the lesson unfolded, Jake's focus shifted. Instead of watching Mrs. P's hands or listening to her advice, he found himself studying Annabelle, who was sitting at the back of the classroom. Her legs were crossed, her hands delicately tucked into the crevices of her thighs. She didn't look away from him, though her eyes fluttered upward toward the ceiling for a brief moment. And then Jake saw it: she was crying. The sight almost made him stop, throw the violin aside, and rush to her. But then, just as quickly, Annabelle smiled softly and laughed quietly to herself. They weren't sad tears. Yet still, Jake felt an overwhelming urge to gently wipe them away from her slender cheeks.

And as Jake played, Mrs. P listened closely. It wasn't perfect—Jake still had a long way to go. He needed to refine his technique, stand a little taller, and lean into the violin more. But there was something different today. Mrs. P could hear it. Jake was playing with something more than just technique. He was playing with heart. Pride swelled in Mrs. P's chest as she recognised the spark in Jake's playing. She knew in that moment that he would be her success story.

The bell rang just thirty seconds after Jake finished. He reached to return the violin to Mrs. P, but she shook her head.

'That violin belongs to no one else but you, Jacob.' She smiled. 'Tonight, go home and show your parents what you've learnt.'

He tried to refuse, but Mrs P was having none of it. Twice she pushed it back into his hands before asking him, no, demanding him to leave her classroom for next period.

'How?' Jake muttered, his palm gripping tightly onto the case as he left the music block.

'How what?' Annabelle asked, walking on his side. They didn't have class together, but neither Annabelle or Jake seemed in a rush to go to their next lesson.

'How am I going to play in front of my parents?' Jake muttered. They had no idea about his secret lessons, no clue about his deep love for the violin or his burning desire to become the world's best violinist.

Annabelle paused. 'Well, how about you play for me instead?' She held up her hand to silence Jake who was ready to question what she meant. 'You *know* you can play in front of me, so let me come and just pretend you're playing in front of me, rather than your parents.'

It was a good idea. He knew he was more than capable of playing in front of Annabelle - in fact he played his best in front of Annabelle, but that meant he had to introduce her to his parents.

'I mean-'

A stern voice belonging to a teacher yelled at the pair to get to lesson, fast.

'I'll wait for you by the gates and we can walk to yours after.' Annabelle hollered over her shoulder. The decision clearly made with or without Jake's input.

It wasn't out of the ordinary for Jake to walk home saying very little, listening to Annabelle delightfully ramble on about her day. She spoke loud and giggled to herself when she relayed moments of her day that she found entertaining, like when her maths teacher spent the lesson teaching with chocolate all over his mouth without having the slightest idea.

'He was- you know, he had it all-' She laughed. 'He looked so *silly!*'

But this time, Jake did not laugh when she did. He could

barely even muster a smile. The weight of his violin in his hand felt like bricks of lead.

'Wowza, are you okay?' Annabelle asked, leaning close to inspect Jake's lips that were almost quivering.

'I'm fine.'

But he wasn't fine. For the first time since their friendship, Annabelle crossed the main road by Jake's side.

'Jake,' Annabelle whispered, her voice barely loud against the zooming cars. 'You'll be okay.'

Jake's father was strict. He held Jake to an incredibly high standard, grafted hard as a mechanic and instilled fear into many people with his naturally stern gaze - everyone except his mother. His father's soft spot for his mother was unlike any other. Jake wasn't surprised to see his parents on the street, the garage door wide open with music blasting from the radio. His father revved the motorbike, with his mother's arms wrapped around him, as they rode up and down the quiet cul-de-sac, laughing.

'Is that- are those your parents?' Annabelle asked. Jake nodded as the pair stood on the pavement listening to the roaring laughter of his mother and watching his father turn the bike sharply around.

'Frank!' Mother said upon noticing Jake and Annabelle watching, waiting. Father rolled to a halt, just a metre away from the pair. 'Jake!' She smiled and then glistened upon looking at Annabelle. 'And who is this lovely girl?' Before Jake could respond, Mother's gaze shifted to the violin in his hands. 'And what's this? Since when–'

But Annabelle stepped forward, extending her hand with a warm smile.

'Hello, Mrs. Robinson. I'm Annabelle.
His mother laughed lightly and shook her hand. His father was smirking by the time she formally reintroduced herself again.

'You must be Jake's friend.' He said.

'I am.' She nodded. 'Actually, I'm his *best friend.*'

'Is that so?' Mother gently touched his arm to silence his deep chuckle. 'Well, Annabelle, I think it's only right that best friends come to tea and have a bit of birthday cake.' Jake didn't hide his grimace in time.

'Birthday?' She shouted. 'It's your–'

'Jake, did you not tell your best friend it's your eleventh birthday today?' Mother shook her head. Annabelle's frown was so sharp it cut Jake almost in half.

'I was going to tell you.' Jake lied. He had absolutely no intention of telling Annabelle it was his birthday. Jake hated many things: loud noises and attention centred on him, all things guaranteed on a birthday. He tried to minimise this at all costs, even if that included lying to his best friend. Blushing at the thought, Jake added, 'I'm sorry.'

His father hopped off his motorbike and then helped his

mother off, gently holding her hand to do so. Jake wished he could hold Annabelle's hand like that. Instead, it was Jake's mother to hold Annabelle by the shoulders and direct her into the house.

'Don't worry, lovely, Jake isn't one to share big news.'

'Talking of big news-' Annabelle said, stalking off with his mother.

Jake tried to prevent Annabelle from saying anything further when he was interrupted by a hefty pat on the back from his father, catching him completely off guard.

'Jake, she seems lovely.'

'She is.'

'And you brought her here on your birthday.' He grinned. Jake was ready to run into the house, but it was his father's words that interrupted him this time. 'I'm proud of you, son.'

Jake had very little time to revel in the moment as his father started to wheel the motorbike toward the opened garage and his mother hollered for him inside.

Watching Annabelle shovelling food in her mouth, questioning his father on the different types of cars he's worked on and then complimenting his mother on her beautiful home, made Jake both nervous and giddy. But he did not expect the loud singing from Annabelle as his mother brought over a vanilla iced cake with exactly eleven candles on top. Annabelle's voice was piercing and his father barely murmured the song through his wide smile. His mother planted a delicate kiss through the scruff of Jake's hair as she lowered the cake in front of him.

'Make a wish, Jake.'

He didn't need to ask for anything specific; silently, he wished that every birthday from now on would be like this one, surrounded by the people he loved.

It was all interrupted, only an hour later by his gasping mother as they stood in the living room, Jake brandishing the violin.

'You're telling me you've been learning the violin this whole time?'

He nodded. The only sound came from the ice cubes in his tumbler of whiskey.

'Mrs Robinson, Jake is honestly amazing. The best musician I've ever seen.'

Unsure how many musicians Annabelle had seen, Jake shook his head. The best musician was sitting on the sofa, nestling next to his father, eyeing the violin with curiosity.

'Are you sure your teacher is happy to give you the instrument, Jake? I mean that thing must be worth at least-'

'Annette,' his father exhaled. 'Just let the boy play, will you?'

She pressed her mouth in a firm line and proceeded to sit back, trying to relax into the cushions. Annabelle sat cross-legged on the floor.

You've got this, she mouthed, putting her thumbs up.

Jake placed his chin into the rest, like he had done many times, but today his fingers shook. Maybe he should practise a bit more. Go back to Mrs P and ask for more rehearsals, but when he breathed and played the first note, he closed his eyes and his shaking fingers steadied. Mrs P told him many times that good musicians do not close their eyes when they play. But today, he could not help it, even with Annabelle's soft gaze, he could not bear to open them.

He played, for how long, he did not know but when the song finished he opened his eyes again. The room was silent. It made Jake's breathing seem deafeningly loud. Tears were running down Mother's face, Annabelle's too and even his father quickly tried to wipe his eyes before Jake noticed his moist cheek. Unsurprisingly, Jake did not know what to say. It was his mother who spoke first.

'Again.' Her eyes glistened. 'Play again.'

With a heavy nod from his father and a kind smile from Annabelle, Jake raised the violin again.

CHAPTER 2
21-22

It took not one but two heavy yanks in an attempt to loosen the bolt, but when it did, oil gushed out thick and fast. Luckily, the bucket Jake placed beneath caught every drop, except the few that splashed onto his blue overalls. It wasn't until the car released the last of its oil, Jake could hear Ritchie yelling his name.

'Get up here, kid.'

When Jake emerged above the car, he took a deep breath of fresh air but he could not remove the fumes that stuck in the back of his throat. Ritchie stood by the edge of the car, holding onto a clip-board

'Kid,' he repeated, gesturing for Jake to come over with a flick of his index finger. Jake knew better than to correct him or leave Ritchie waiting. He wasn't really a kid anymore, not when he towered over people twice his age, his voice deep and monotone, each word spoken in measured syllables.

'Here you go.' Ritchie pulled an envelope from the clip-board. Even from arm's length, Jake could see its thin contents. He made a certain effort not to show frustration in front of Ritchie. The man was a saint after all. Most employers would've got rid of Jake the first month after his mother's diagnosis, let alone taking a year off to stay at home to become her full-time carer. But the thin envelope that sat in his hand was not at fault of his sick mother.

'You good, son?' Ritchie eyed Jake.

'Yes, sir.' Jake smiled. 'I'll shift my weight this month, I promise.'

Ritchie shook his head, 'You do what you gotta' do. There will always be a place for you under this roof. I owe your father that much.'

The mention of his father made Jake stiffen. Ritchie had worked alongside his father for years at the shop, and it was Ritchie who first noticed how things spiralling out of control. He had seen it before Jake did—the way his father's drinking had taken over, the same way the illness had gradually drained the life out of his mother. Jake thought of the mornings when his father woke up drunk, and went to sleep the same. It all came to a head after a violent altercation a year ago with a colleague, one that left Ritchie with no choice but to fire him.

Jake knew the moment it happened, things would change. But Ritchie had never been the type to leave anyone hanging. With the bills piling up and the mortgage looming, Jake stepped in. He didn't have a choice, he knew enough about the trade to keep his family afloat, even if he had never imagined he'd be the one holding it all together.

'How is he?' Ritchie asked, hugging the board to his chest now. 'He doin' alright?'

Only last night, Jake walked in after a twelve hour shift to find his father passed out on the sofa with vomit down his clothes. The smell continued to linger in Jake's nose.

'Better.' Jake's smile did not waver.

Ritchie nodded, 'Good, good.' He didn't buy it, not for even a moment, but he still gave Jake the grace by pretending to. 'Things are looking good down here. Go take your lunch break.'

'No, no, I'll-'

Ritchie didn't argue, instead he narrowed his eyebrows and that was enough to silence Jake. So, he grabbed his ham and mustard sandwiches with the bread he picked mould off in the morning and decided he would go for a walk rather than sit in the tea room.

The sun beat down on him as he strolled, folding the bread into his mouth and chewing. There wasn't much to do, other than stroll and take a seat on the bench that overlooked a particularly green lake. He wished he bought his violin but he trusted no one at the shop enough to leave it unattended. Still, he couldn't help but feel he could have used this time to practice for his performance tonight.

With working long hours, looking after his father and passing out in bed from exhaustion, Jake had very little time to even contemplate tonight's performance, which in hindsight was incredibly stupid of him. Tonight was important. It could get him the scholarship of a lifetime; enrol him into Eldenford University where his music could take him places he could never go before. So, when he sat on the bench, looking at the emerald algae ahead, Jake thought of the notes, practiced the placement of his fingers on the strings, and imagined the roaring success of his performance. As he focused, he felt a strange emptiness settle within him. At some point, his eyes closed, and in the darkness behind his eyelids, he no longer saw the bustling audience he had pictured. Instead, he saw the empty chair in the front row—cold, unmoving, and vacant. That chair had been empty for months now, a silent reminder that his mother had passed before he even received the invitation to perform.

Jake's eyes snapped open and with a shaking hand, he reached for the cartoon of cigarettes in his pocket. It was sometime between putting the cigarette in his mouth and patting his overalls, he realised he left his lighter at the shop.

'Dammit.'

When Jake first sat down, the lake was empty, offering no opportunity to light his cigarette. He'd almost resigned himself to waiting when, out of the corner of his eye, he saw a figure moving slowly along the lake, a cloud of smoke swirling around her. He didn't think much of it at first, but then, as the figure in a luscious violet dress drew closer, he caught sight of her face. He blinked, rubbed his eyes, and leaned forward so suddenly he almost toppled off the bench. It was Annabelle.

He hadn't seen her in a long, long time, and here she was, standing right before him.

'Well, as I live and breathe.' Annabelle broke the stillness first, her voice light but with an unmistakable warmth. 'Jakey.'

Her gaze softened, and before Jake could react, she stepped forward, her arms wide open, but he jerked back instinctively, almost too quickly.

'Oil,' Jake muttered, his cigarette still perched between his lips, unlit and dangling like an afterthought.

'What?' Annabelle asked, confused for a moment, but then her eyes flicked down to his stained overalls, and a small, knowing smile tugged at the corner of her lips. 'Oh, I see.' With a flick of her wrist, she pulled a Zippo lighter from her bag, the metal gleaming in the dim light. The smoke caught in his throat as she lit it for him and he resisted the urge to cough.

'What's it been? Three years?' Annabelle asked.
Three years had passed since Jake had last said farewell to Annabelle. A university by the coast had lured her away, offering her the chance to become a nurse, a dream she'd held for as long as Jake had known her. She left with her bright eyes full of ambition, leaving Jake behind in the same town, stuck in a cycle of responsibility. While she pursued her future, Jake stayed, putting a pause on his own dreams, his own desires. He'd stepped into the role of caregiver for his mother, watching her health slowly decline, and worked tirelessly in the mechanic's shop, fixing cars just like his

father had taught him. The years blurred into one another, and with every turn of the wrench.

'Yes, three years,' he repeated, as if confirming the reality of it all.

Jake studied Annabelle as she spoke. He could see it in her eyes, the quiet acknowledgment of all the lost promises, the things they swore they would never let slip away: the letters, the phone calls, the promises of staying in touch no matter where life took them. But time had a way of stealing those promises, of wearing them down until they were nothing more than fading memories. Annabelle's gaze flickered across the lake, and she gestured with a soft hand.

'I'm here to see Lottie, actually.'

Jake nodded, trying to suppress the small pang of something, disappointment, maybe, or simply the awareness that they had both moved on, in different directions, and were now standing on different paths.

'That's nice,' he replied, though the words felt hollow in his mouth.

Her hands moved to ends of her hair, fiddling absentmindedly. It was short, much shorter than Jake remembered, a neat, tousled bob that framed her face in a way that seemed both familiar and foreign. She had always wanted it that length, but her mother had insisted on keeping it longer, saying it suited her better. Jake wondered what else had changed, things that weren't immediately obvious - those little quirks that once made her, her. Did she still snort when she laughed too loudly, the kind of laugh that always seemed to catch her off guard? Did she still whistle when she was lost in thought, a tune only she could hear, her mind wandering as her fingers fidgeted with anything in reach? He suddenly realised how much he missed the details, the small, unique parts of her that seemed to fade into the background when they'd drifted apart.

'So, tell me.' She breathed. 'How's mum and dad? Dad still on those bikes? Mum asking him to get off and help her with dinner?' Her laughter was hearty, as if the memory of Jake's family were only yesterday.

'Ma passed away seven months ago.'

He wanted to cushion it and say it gently, but the words came out harsh and hard. The cigarette in her hand became limp and the smoke expelled from her lips before it even had time to reach her lungs. He didn't have time to warn her again. Oil would definitely stain her beautiful violet dress, but she pulled him into a hug all the same.

'Damn Lottie,' Annabelle cursed as she stepped out of the hug, but remained close to Jake's body. 'Of all the things she tells me about.' She took a hearty drag of her cigarette and Jake followed suit. It shouldn't have surprised Jake to see the tears swell into Annabelle's eyes. She loved his mother like most of the town did - fiercely, with a deep need to protect her. He wanted to apologise for not informing her of her passing, but in the corner of his eye, he noticed the time ticking away.

'I've got to go.' He stubbed his cigarette out, gathering his rubbish from the bench, his movements quick as he prepared to dash back to work. But just before he turned, the words slipped out, more out of the hope that their paths would cross again than anything else.

'What are you doing tonight, Ann?'

The question lingered between them, and for a moment, he felt a pang of disappointment. He hadn't wanted to leave things like this. He'd hoped for more, more time, more of her.

'Oh, well I was…' She paused, shook her head and smiled. 'Actually, nothing. Why?'

'I'm performing tonight at the City Hall. It's a scholarship thing.' Jake explained quickly. 'It would be great to see you there. It starts at 7.'

'Absolutely, I'll be there.'

It was Jake's turn to pull Annabelle into a hug. She smelt fresh, like washing hung up outside on a warm summer's day. He wanted to hold her for longer. It was nice to know that some things never change.

Condensation blurred the mirror, streaming over flecks of hardened toothpaste clinging stubbornly to the glass. The droplets distorted Jake's reflection, making it appear as though tears were streaming down his face. His shirt was tight and his fingers trembled as he attempted to redo his tie for the third time. The barber had cut his hair far too short, trimmed it at the sides too thin. His mother would've hated it. She would've told him he looked like a skinhead and that no one should be able to see someone's scalp. Shrouded in a memory of his mother, Jake didn't notice his father open the bathroom door and sway beneath the arch. It was the stench of whiskey that gave his presence away.

'Do you need the bathroom?' Jake asked, giving up on his tie and letting it hang around his neck like a scarf. His father stepped in, his fingers also shaking and reached for the burgundy material, tucking it beneath Jake's collar. His bloodshot eyes were barely open and his unsteady feet rocked side-to-side. Yet still, he managed to fold Jake's tie precisely in all the right places and pull it closely to his son's neck, cushioning it gently against Jake's Adam's apple.

'Will I see you there?' Jake asked.

'I wouldn't miss it for the world.' he replied, licking his cracked, pale lips. 'This one's the big one, right?'

Jake nodded.

'Well then, you better get going.' His father said, patting him on the back. In an attempt to leave, his father swayed and

Jake instinctively reached out, grabbing his elbow to steady him. There was a fleeting moment where Jake's heart twisted with a mix of frustration and something softer—a longing, perhaps, for the warmth and stability his mother used to provide. Without thinking, he pulled his father into a hug.

'I love you, dad,' Jake muttered into a head of thinning hair.

'I love you too, son.' His father straightened up, as if the contact had somehow sobered him up. 'Your mother would be so proud.'

The sound of her name hovered between the two men until Jake could not bear it anymore and left the bathroom. He grabbed his violin case, his jacket and refused to look at the grand piano that stood untouched in the middle of the room.

Puberty hit Jake like a train when he turned thirteen. It was as if one night, he had sprouted from 5ft to 6ft. His Adam's apple bulged from his throat and the sickly sweet sound of a young boy's voice was replaced by a husky man's. But it did not change the young school boy's fear that sat in his bones. It presented itself no longer by quivering, but by sweating. That's why, stood by the edge of the stage, glancing between the two-hundred seats and the raised platform, he had no choice but to pull his handkerchief from his pocket and dab the sweat from his brow.

A loud vibration emitted from the hall adjacent to the stage where people mingled, warming up for the performances. And while Jake knew he should join the party, introduce himself to the professors who would decide his fate, Jake knew his personality would not be the way to win them over. They would not be impressed by his never-evolving timid nature. They would find no interest in his stories, for he had none to tell. Who wanted to hear about a drunk father and a dead mother? Undoubtedly, the mingling would be accompanied by champagne and other poison. The prospect of alcohol revulsed Jake. Seeing his father covered in his own vomit over the past few months only deepened the shame Jake had.

Jake slipped out the fire exit and into the dark alleyway that was littered with empty beer bottles and discarded newspapers. He pulled a super-king from his metallic case, the cigarette tip glowing as he lit it. Beneath the harsh, flickering light of a streetlamp, a slender woman emerged from the shadows, her silhouette framed by the dim glow.

'How is it that-' Annabelle chuckled. 'Even after three years of not seeing you I knew you'd be here, tucked away and not chatting away with the others?' The way her navy dress hugged her body nearly made Jake choke on the smoke. Her hair was pinned and a dark rouge stained her peony lips.

'People are loud.'

'Well, unlucky you.' She shrugged, putting her hand on her hips. 'I'm the loudest one out of them all.'

'And the most beautiful.'

The compliment made Annabelle straighten and her

cheeks flush red. She coughed the comment away. 'Are you ready for this?'

'As ready as I'll ever be.'

'Well, if you're as good as I remember, you'll blow them all away.' She winked. 'You belong on that stage.'

'With you in the wing, right?'

A distant promise made by young teenagers hovered between them. Annabelle could only bring herself to nod.

A darkened lamp mounted onto the brick wall, suddenly burst to life and flashed five times. It was time. Jake grabbed his case, stubbed out the smoked cigarette and opened the fire exit door.

'Don't forget to breathe, alright?' Her voice was steady, but there was a quiet warmth in it that made Jake pause.

He raised an eyebrow, a small smile tugging at the corner of his mouth. 'Breathe, huh?'

She nodded, her eyes soft. 'Yeah, breathe. You've got this, Jake.'

'Enjoy the show, Ann.'

Annabelle's loud wishes of luck trailed behind.

It's always sad when something that is supposed to be so great, so meaningful, so poignant, is overshadowed by seething disappointment. Jake prepared himself and to some degree accepted, before walking into the spotlight, that he would not see his mother sat on the front row. He did not expect his father's seat to be empty too. He did not know why he hadn't considered that a possibility. Jake was let down by his father many times: no shows at dinners, too busy curling himself into a corner of the pub. Smaller, lesser performances he did not make as he fell asleep on his recliner at home. So when Jake's fingers rested on the strings, and his chin laid on its rest, he thought of his father. For the whole performance, Jake thought of no one else. He imagined going home, smashing those whiskey bottles against the wall and screaming into his face.

The grief, the disappointment, the pain flooded into each note and that is why Jake played his best ever performance.

His bow struck the strings with ferocity, the sound was a cry that reverberated through the air. The melody swelled, teetering between something beautiful and something indescribably haunting. His fingers trembled but never faltered, gripping the fingerboard like a lifeline, dragging aching harmonies from depths he did not know existed. The sound rose in a crescendo, sharp and piercing, then broke into a tormenting lament, echoing.

The last note hung in the air, trembling, as if it had nowhere else to go. The room silent, and then – clapping. At first, it was tentative, polite. But then, as if some unspoken signal passed between them, the audience erupted into hysteria. The sound swelled around him, loud and immense, bouncing off the walls, filling his chest. Jake looked down at his violin, his hands still hovering in the aftermath, and only then did he allow himself to acknowledge the loud cry. The audience were on their feet now, applauding, but his eyes, almost instinctively, sought her out. And there she was, in the middle row, her hands clasped together, her face flushed. She was clapping harder than anyone else, her tears shimmering in the dim lights. It hit him then, how much he had missed her. A hollow space he hadn't realised he'd been carrying all this time

Backstage, he didn't expect it. She was there, waiting for him, just like she'd always said she would be when they were children. How she managed to slip past security, he would never know. But, at that moment, it didn't matter. Annabelle ran straight into his arms, a fierce urgency in her embrace. Before Jake could even process the warmth of her body against his, her lips found his. The kiss was deep and full of yearning, a hunger he hadn't known she harboured, one that surprised him and left him breathless. Her hands tangled in his hair, pulling him closer, and for the first time, Jake understood – truly understood – the kind of love he had held for her all this time. A waited, patient kind of love. He didn't care how she had gotten there, or what security had said. In that kiss, everything else fell away.

'You were amazing, Jake!' Tears were still in her eyes. He held her by the dip in her spine. 'My god, you were-'
This time, he kissed her. The grief, the disappointment, the

pain – it all disappeared.

'Are you sure you don't want to stay?' Annabelle asked, pointing at the City Hall behind her, her other hand firmly planted in his.

'I can't,' Jake said, whistling a cab down. He had to go home, he had to see his father. Slowly, a figure emerged from the town hall's doors. He thought he had seen enough light emerge from the shadows tonight; the brightest still holding onto his palm, he did not expect to see another. It was Annabelle who said her name first.

'Mrs P.'

She held onto a walking stick and her knees wobbled as she walked down the steps to her old pupil. Jake could not remember the last time he even thought of her.

'You were fantastic tonight, Jacob.'

He hadn't heard that name in years, twelve, to be exact. The shift from 'small' school to 'big' school had quietly severed their connection. Mrs. P had given him more than just a violin over the years; she'd gifted him kindness, patience, and the belief that he could become someone more than what he had been.

The taxi driver hollered out the open window.

'We have to go.' Jake muttered. 'My father–'

'Go.' Mrs P nodded. There was familiarity in her instruction. 'I know I shouldn't be the one to tell you this, but… you got it.' Her smile was soft.

'Got what?' Jake asked, but again it was Annabelle who spoke first.

'Oh my god, *the scholarship!*' Annabelle squeezed his hand before pulling Jake into a hug. But Jake's eyes remained fixated on Mrs P who stood glowing in front of the double doors of the hall. It didn't feel strange when he left Annabelle's embrace and hugged his old teacher.

'Professor Baker's an old friend of mine,' Mrs. P said, her voice low and warm. 'I didn't mention you were one of my students, but when she saw you perform... well, she knew right away.' She chuckled softly. 'They absolutely loved you, Jacob.' Mrs P pulled away and patted him on the arms. 'Now go.'

Jake nearly choked on his words. 'I owe it all to you, Mrs P.'

'No-no, young man, that was all you.'

The driver threatened to leave, so Jake hurried away. He nestled into the back, Annabelle leaning close to his body.

Jake should've been doing two things: basking in the glory of his successful performance and kissing Annabelle. Instead, he stared out the window of the moving car, stiff, his fingers picking at the skin around his callouses.

'Is it your dad?' Annabelle asked. Her thumb tracing the indent of Jake's wrist.

He nodded. If he spoke, he would cry or yell and he didn't

know what was worse.

'Hey,' Annabelle's gentle fingers coaxed Jake's cheeks, forcing him to look at her. 'Talk to me.'

'Since Mum's death, Dad's been—' The embarrassment rose in his gut. 'He's not well.'

'You're disappointed he didn't come tonight.'

He almost laughed. 'You know, on that stage, that is the closest I've ever got to feeling like I hate him.' Jake expected her to insist that it was not true because, of course, it wasn't. Jake loved his father, idolised him even, but Annabelle soothed him when she said,

'That's understandable.' Her eyes not moving from his. 'Maybe you need to tell him how you feel. Maybe tonight is the night things change for everyone.'

Jake agreed. So, for the remainder of the journey, he thought of what he would say to his father. He would tell his dad that he missed Mum too, but no matter how painful it was, the world continued to spin. He would tell him how it felt as though he had lost two parents in one and that he desperately wanted his father back now. Everything he wanted to say for the past seven months was now on the tip of his tongue.

But little did Jake know, he would never tell his father any of it.

Instead, when he walked into the house, with Annabelle by his side, he would see his father half dressed in his tux, his tie wrapped around his cold fingers, collapsed onto the floor. His body wet from an upturned bottle of whiskey that rolled itself next to the legs of the piano. He would watch as Annabelle started chest compressions in a desperate, but futile attempt, to revive his father. It would take not one, nor two but three attempts for Annabelle to command Jake to call an ambulance. He would not remember speaking to the operator. But he would learn how violent chest compressions look on a lifeless body. The sound of his father's ribs breaking would force him to intervene with a howling cry, demanding Annabelle to stop. And he would pry his father from her grip, the unworn tie wrapping itself around Jake's hand, to just hold him tight and cry.

The wood moulded itself into Jake's spine and the echoes of the priest's voice rolled in his skull. People all around him cried, all except Annabelle who did her best to stifle her tears. She wiped them when she thought he wasn't looking and she choked on her sobs in an attempt to hide them. Jake said nothing, did nothing. His duty had been carrying his father's casket as he did his mother's, not even a year before.

The wake was no different. Jake accepted condolences from faces he recognised, and shook hands with those who regarded his father a great man - not the drunk he had become. When Jake trailed towards the bathroom, unable to watch those pick up a drink in his father's honour, Annabelle followed after him.

'Hey, wait up.' Annabelle called. He ignored her, reaching the bathroom doors asking her to stop.

'Stop what?'

'Stop acting like you can't be sad around me.' He didn't let her reply. Instead, he walked into the gents, straight to the basin and ran the cold water, splashing his face repeatedly until his cheeks were numb. He was surprised to see Annabelle standing behind him in the reflection of the mirror.

'What are you doing?' Jake asked, looking at the empty urinals.

'I'm trying to help.'

And she had. From the moment they found his father's body, Annabelle never left his side. She took on everything—the funeral arrangements, from the caterers to the flowers—while balancing her job at the hospital. She managed her own grief, his grief, and the heavy, suffocating grief that filled his parents' house, where they stayed together. There were nights when she cooked dinner, even though Jake barely had the energy to care, his hunger replaced by nothing more than the need for a cigarette.

'Not being sad isn't helping.' Jake didn't know why he was saying these words, but his fingers gripped the porcelain skin until his knuckles turned white.

'I *am* sad,' she breathed. 'But I'm also looking after you.' She closed the gap between them and the faint trace of her sweet perfume lingered. Even at a funeral, she was the most beautiful woman he'd ever seen. The elegance of her slicked back hair and the black dress made him weak. This was not how Jake imagined their relationship. He never thought, not for one moment, that the same day they shared their first kiss - which they would of course reminisce about in years to come - would be the same day they found his father…

'I do not need looking after.'

'Yes, you do.'

'No, I do not!' He yelled. 'Just back off, will you?!' It was the first time Annabelle ever heard him yell. It was also the first time he'd heard himself yell, and he hated it. He hated the sharp edge of his voice, how it carried so far, reverberating off the cold, sterile tiles of the room. He expected Annabelle to tell him to calm down, to wait until he had cooled off and they could talk, just like his mother used to do with his father. Instead, Annabelle stepped even closer. Her voice was the softest he had ever heard it,

'You've spent years looking after someone.' Her words calm but laced with heaviness. 'Now it's your turn to be looked after, Jake. Let someone take care of you for once.'

But she wasn't just *someone*. It was Annabelle who stood in front of him, wanting to help, just as she had helped a decade ago, prying those bullies from him. Yet still, as if it were a reflex, Jake shook his head and muttered beneath his breath that he was fine. Her cold hands held his face. Her index finger tracing the heavy bags beneath his eyes.

'No, you're not fine. You're sad and you're angry, angry that they're gone, sad that they're not coming back, but it's okay. It's okay to feel that.'

The rise in his chest caught in his throat and hot tears reached the surface of his eyes. They rolled down Annabelle's fingers.

'I… I just can't believe they're gone.' Jake whispered. He fell into her hold as if he were once again a small child. 'They're gone and they've left me here all alone.' He cried into her neck and she held him upright as his knees threatened to buckle.

'You're not alone,' she whispered into his ear. Her words warm. He realised that she too was crying. 'You have me, Jake. You'll never, ever be alone.'

Time moved differently for Jake after his father's death. It consisted of doing the things he needed to do; wake up, brush his teeth, shower, eat and of course work at the garage. It wasn't too dissimilar of a time after his mother died. But instead of looking after his withered drunken father, he spent his free time packing his parents' belongings, selling them or discarding them where necessary. It continued to pass, as time always does. But it was hard to comprehend how easily day became night and night became day.

Annabelle's presence made it easier. Her laughter at his silly jokes made the hardness inside of him soft, and she too managed to pry a chuckle from his lips. She would come in from a twelve hour shift at the hospital, looking how she had when she left the house with a deep sense of joy and appreciation for being able to help those in need. They would have dinner together, always, no matter how late she trailed in. He would play her songs on the violin, and she would sit there and listen.

No one ever questioned how quickly Annabelle found her way into Jake's life and how effortlessly he fit into hers. Not her parents, not her friends, not even Lottie, who had since moved on and found a boyfriend, no longer carrying a fondness for Jake. It was simply understood by everyone around them, even though they had once failed to see their undeniable connection, the way they seemed to orbit each other without even trying. And Jake wasn't resentful about the three years they had lost; after all, who knew what might have happened in that time? He couldn't imagine Annabelle falling into his life in any other way, but in a time of deep need.

And in return, she revealed she had needed him too. University had been a long and gruelling journey for her, full of late nights and endless deadlines. The work was demanding, and at times, she went to bed hungry, never able to ask her parents for another loan, despite their wealth. It was in those moments of vulnerability that they discovered the depth of their bond, the unspoken understanding that they were there for each other when no one else could be.

And so, in a rare moment of peace, as she made them pancakes on their first Saturday off in a long time, he told her that he was venturing into the garage. The sunlight beamed into the kitchen as Annabelle, wearing one of Jake's shirts, cracked an egg into the bowl.

'Would you like me to help?' She asked, pausing before putting the shells in the bin.

'I got this.' He replied, kissing her on the cheek.

The garage air was cold, stagnant despite the breeze blowing calmly outside. Time seemed to move everywhere, but here, the collected dust made sure of it. In an attempt to bring it back to life, Jake turned the light and radio on. The light flickered and the sound crackled, but a series of songs started playing in the background. The bike was hidden beneath a grey sheet and Jake disturbed the dust as he removed it. The fibres that circled in the air did not move the memories that came with it. His father loved this bike, admired it. It was the same way Jake looked at his violin, but now the bike seemed smaller. The metal cold to touch.

'Jake,' her voice made him jump. She treaded into the garage, barefoot, still only in his shirt.

'Anne, be careful there's glass and debris on the–'
She brandished a white envelope.

'The postman just came,' she announced, holding it up. 'It's for you.'

The stamp was large, displaying the institution's name with pride. With everything that happened, Jake had placed the scholarship to the back of his mind, unable to think of his success without it holding hands with his grief.

'Open it,' Annabelle instructed.
So he did. He was congratulated, warmly, on his scholarly success and the university was excited to offer a scholarship to such a talented musician. And, when Annabelle bound into his arms, as she had done the night of his performance, yelling her praises, in the mix of it all, she said,

'I love you! I'm so in love with you!'
It was the first time those words were exchanged and although Jake had thought of it, wanted to say it even, of course it would be Annabelle - in all her brazen glory - who would say it first. But it would be him, holding onto the letter, onto her, who would say, without thinking, with no preparation at all,

'Marry me, Annabelle.'

She froze, her eyes wide. The words hung in the air between them. Then, slowly, a soft laugh escaped her lips, almost nervously, as she stepped back slightly, her hands still resting on his shoulders.

'Jake...' she whispered, her voice barely above a breath. The kiss was sudden, but it was filled with the quiet certainty of everything they'd been through together, a wordless answer to the question that had caught her off guard. To steady them both, his hands held her so tightly he almost tore the letter in two.

'Annabelle, you gotta' actually say yes, you know that right?' He laughed, not quite believing he was commanding her to talk, but of course, when she said yes, she yelled it. She yelled it so loud Jake was convinced that wherever his parents were they would've heard it too. The radio continued to crackle so loud that they could not distinguish the song that was playing, but Annabelle placed her delicate toes on top of Jake's feet and they danced in each other's arms.

Little did Jake realise, until later that day, he had asked Annabelle to marry him on a beautiful spring day. The air was warm and flowers were sprouting in beds of grass as the pair walked together through town.

'Should we tell people?' Annabelle asked, squeezing Jake's hand.

'Maybe we should wait.' Jake replied, kissing her bare hand. 'I didn't even get round to asking your father-'

'Father shmather.' Annabelle rolled her eyes. 'I don't need his permission to love you.'

'Well, I still-'

'Oh my god!' Annabelle said in a loud, and failed, whisper, pulling Jake to a halt. 'Is that *Marco*?' The name took Jake by surprise, but he followed Annabelle's indiscreet pointed stare to see a stocky man with broad shoulders and dark beard standing at the bus stop. 'Wow, he looks… different.'

They must have been staring a bit too long because, before Jake could respond, Marco caught sight of them. His eyes flicked to them, and a soft smile spread across his face - one Jake had never seen before, not in their younger years.

'Should we… should we go say hi?' Annabelle waved back. Jake made no effort to return his kind gesture. Instead, he shook his head and again reached for Annabelle's hand. Some things—and some people—were better left in the past. Deep down, Jake knew that without Marco's torment, he might never have found Annabelle. But he couldn't bring himself to give Marco credit for the ugly things that had ultimately led to something so beautiful. Jake pulled Annabelle into his arms and in the dip of her neck told her he wanted to marry her this summer.

Jake spent an evening curled up on the sofa, looking at the laminated and bounded folder that Annabelle crafted to plan their wedding. He did not question her wants or desires for the day, but he did listen. He listened and agreed when she chose white peonies for their flowers. He nodded when she revealed her bridesmaids, and even chuckled when she said Lottie would be her maid of honour.

'What about you? Who's your best man?'

Jake tried to hide the embarrassment when he realised his options on groomsmen, let alone a best man, would be limited.

'Ritchie,' he had said, hoping his boss at the garage would accept. And, of course, he had.

Time and time again, Annabelle suggested they scale back the wedding—asked if they should opt for something smaller, something more within a reasonable budget. But Jake dismissed her concerns each time. He couldn't bear the thought of cutting corners on what should be a special day for her. So, he worked extra shifts at the garage to bring in more money, and when that wasn't enough, he was both surprised and relieved when Annabelle's father, who had more than enough to spare, offered to cover half of the costs.

'Only because she's marrying you, sonny!' he had chuckled. 'If it were anyone else, I'd tell 'em to stick it.' Jake had wanted to argue, to say the financial help should be about his daughter's happiness, not his approval. But the words didn't come. Instead, he graciously accepted the cheque, thanking him with a sincerity that made his discomfort easier to swallow.

The tiredness and shame was always a lot easier when he heard Annabelle giggling. Just like she was doing on the phone to Lottie, the same evening when Jake received a letter from Eldenford. It was a list, an extensive one at that, comprised of several songs and composers. All things he was set to study in preparation for his first term come September. Jake recognised most of the composers but, worryingly, only a few of the songs. He had been playing the violin as often as he could, often stalking off the garage late at night, unwilling to keep Annabelle up when she had a morning shift at the hospital.

'What's that?' Annabelle's voice caught him off guard. He didn't hear her say goodbye to Lottie and when he lifted the paper, she gently pried it from his fingers. Her smile was instantaneous. 'This is exciting.' She studied his face. 'You're excited, right?'

'I am.' Jake confirmed. 'But I have more important pressing matters at hand.' He smiled, taking the paper from her hand and letting it float to the ground.

'Oh, yeah?' She giggled. 'Is that so?'

'Abso-' He kissed her. '-lutely.'

'And what pressing matter may that be?' Her fingers crawled through the thickness of his hair as she stood on her pointed toes.

'Marrying my best friend.'

She gasped. 'Jake Robinson, are you telling me I'm just a *friend-*'

He did not let her finish her sentence. Instead, he swept her into his arms, mindlessly stepping over the letter in the process.

Yet on the night of their wedding, where it was considered bad luck to see the bride before the big day and it would be appropriate to get an early night, Jake and Annabelle stayed up late, laughing, smoking, calling each other *Mr and Mrs*.

It was almost 3am when Annabelle pointed to the piano and asked him to play. The instrument was regularly dusted and tuned, but never played. The request made him think of his mother and how his father would watch her, a drink in hand. The memory once would've made him sad, but maybe it was because he was a little delirious at 3am or maybe it was because he was marrying the love of his life, he sat down on the stool like his mother had done countless times. When his finger struck the first chord, he realised that his parents deserved to be remembered beyond the years or months leading to their deaths. Their illness, and the tumultuous time it brought with it, was only a fraction of the years they had spent adoring each other, adoring Jake. So, he played. He played what he could remember from his mother's song, which he realised when he finished, was all of it.

'Let's go to bed,' Jake said to the silent room and that's when he noticed that Annabelle had fallen asleep. He pried the blanket from her body, scooped her in his arms and carried her to their bed.

He will, until death, remember every moment of their wedding. How Annabelle's dream had become a fleshed reality - from the catering, to the flowers, to the dresses and music. But all Jake would ever tell anyone who asked about their special day was the moment Annabelle, with her father in hand, walked down the aisle.. Her blonde hair was curled, the dress hanging perfectly from her slender shoulders, the sleeves gently resting on her steady hands. There was no fear in her, nothing could evoke fear in a woman like her. The veil trailed behind her, almost as long as the dress itself, with flowers woven into the fabric that seemed to know they belonged only to Annabelle. Annabelle belonged to no one, not her father, who passed her hand to Jake, and certainly not to Jake himself. No one could ever handle a woman born to be free, to never be tamed. The space she occupied was hers alone; Jake was just fortunate enough to stand in it beside her. So, that's when he told her, when it was his turn to speak, that he would love her forever. That his love for her lived in the smallest things, making her coffee in the morning, her sleepy chamomile tea at night. That his love for her was like a song that had no end and would keep playing until the end of time. And that when times get tough, as they undoubtedly would, he would continue to choose her. Choose her every time the sun rose and the sun set.

By the time it was her turn, she was whispering about a love that was loud, unapologetic, and never-ending. A love that would keep him full, always in abundance, no matter what came their way. Then they kissed and their promises were sealed until death to they part.

The train journey was chaotic. People were wedged into the carriage, seemingly unbothered as they traversed like cattle into the city. Jake recognised no one. They all donned business attire that Jake had only seen in shop windows and on television. They sipped on their morning coffees, knowing all the appropriate intervals of movement to do so without spilling their hot drink down their flashy clothes. Jake clung onto his case in one hand and a note in the other.

Annabelle left for work before him. He spent all night looking over the books he had already read for his first day. He went to sleep so late and hadn't even stirred in the morning until his alarm beeped at him to wake up. Annabelle's note was on the kitchen table and in her rushed and, admittedly, horrible handwriting, she wished him luck on his first day at university. It marked a new beginning, it wrote, for us both.

Although Jake hoped that the train journey would have consisted of him staring out the window, watching the rolling fields and waking summer morning, he stood next to the toilets, crammed in the corner. Jake lost his footing and nearly tumbled backwards where a girl was huddled on the floor.

'Sorry!' Jake wheezed, fearing his big feet had caught her.

'All good, my friend.' She smiled. There was something comedic, watching this girl with shaved head and a gold tooth, brandish a harmonica from her handbag and say, 'Fancy a tune?' She played one note before the ticket conductor on the other side of the carriage yelled,

'Not today Mona!'

The comment made her laugh, and she rolled her eyes.

'Some people, ay?'

The train arrived at Eldenford and it took a long while for everyone to exit, but once Jake had, he took a large deep breath of fresh air.

It took Jake nearly half an hour to find his way from the station to St. Eldates, and even when he did, he was unsure he was at the right place. The buildings in Eldenford were all similar and Jake spent another three minutes walking up and down, not realising he was in front of the building he both wanted and needed.

It wasn't until the woman with the gold tooth and shaved head waltzed up to Jake, munching on a croissant, pointing behind him.

'Faculty of Music?' She asked, food spitting from her mouth. Jake nodded. 'Right there.'

'Oh, right, thank you.' And as he hurried down the footpath, sweat creeping onto his brow, he realised the girl was at his heels.

'I knew you were a musician,' she laughed. 'I could tell.' Jake looked at the violin case in his hand unimpressed, ignoring the remnants of croissant caught in her teeth. 'Let me guess… you look like a trombone player…' She hummed as they entered the doors together. 'Yet you carry a case for a violin perhaps?' The air in the building smelt of coffee and pamphlet paper. 'My initial deductions have failed me so it seems.'

Jake always wondered how, being as quiet as he was, he always attracted the talkative people.

'I'm sorry,' he breathed, looking at the empty reception desk. 'It's my first day, so I must enrol.'

'Mine too!' She said enthusiastically, not quite catching his tone. 'The name is Mona. A bit like Mona Lisa - actually, exactly like Mona Lisa, the nuns at the orphanage were art fanatics you see.' Mona extended her hand and, fumbling slightly, Jake shook it.

'Jake.' He said.

'You know all we have to do is register at Silverwood Hall, right?' She added. Jake did not know that, but before he could ask, she stormed ahead. 'Follow me!'

So he did, this time inches from her heels. She was in no way, shape or form, like Annabelle. She stomped in heavy Doc Martins and was dressed head-to-toe in black, a large heavy leather jacket dragging from her shoulders.

'I think… I believe it is this way.' She hummed, walking down the hall.

Just as Jake was about to stop, give up on this eccentric woman and her peculiar ways, they were greeted by a warm smile and an open set of double doors.

'First years?' The man said, wearing a grey shirt and a lanyard that read: STUDENT REP. The guy asked for their names and checked Jake and Mona off a list and it was as easy as that. They were enrolled at Eldenford University.

'Got you panicked there for a sec, didn't I?' Mona laughed. Although Jake did find the comment rather humorous, he became silent as he was met by the most beautiful hall he had ever gazed upon. They were surrounded by red benches that all stared ahead at the black grand piano, and standing in the centre of it all was one of the professors who had watched Jake in the town hall many moons ago.

'Welcome. I'm Professor Baker. Please, do take a seat.' She looked older than he remembered. He probably did too. Back then he was merely a boy on a stage, now he was a married man, aged by time and grief.

As Jake settled onto the bench, he noticed a scattering of people throughout the hall, perhaps eight or so, though he didn't bother to count. He placed the violin carefully between his feet, feeling the coolness of the case beneath his fingers. Mona slipped quietly into the space beside him.

The acoustics of the hall were beautiful, so it was no surprise when Professor Baker revealed that this venue was thought to be the first custom built concert-hall, opening its doors in 1747.

'We will not be in here as often as you may like.' The professor laughed. 'Today is manufactured to show you the wonders Eldenford can provide for you - if you apply yourselves and showcase your unruly talent.' Behind her specs, she looked at Jake. 'For most of your days here, you will be in an ordinary classroom, sitting on ordinary seats. Or finding comfort in the library, preparing all the wonderful work you shall produce.'

Jake wished Annabelle were with him. Instead, he sat next to Mona, who twirled the ring in her nose round and round again.

'You will become intimate with one and another in this hall. You will learn what makes each musician in this room tick, and in order to do exactly that we must first know each other's names and instruments to truly get a sense of character.' Professor Baker said, pulling a piece of paper that perched on top of the grand piano. 'Nicholas Anderson, you shall go first.'

The boy in the first row stood, his posture straight as if he were already at home in Eldenford. If anyone embodied the essence of the place, it was Nicholas. Dressed from head to toe in tweed, he introduced himself with practiced precision, listing off the instruments he played—five, in total. Jake's hand began to tremble as Nicholas continued, his fingers tightening around the violin resting by his feet. He hadn't prepared himself for this level of talent, and heat rushed to his cheeks.

The next person, Beatrice Candar, stood and unveiled her own impressive collection of skills - again, plural. Jake felt himself shrink further into his seat, the weight of the expectations pressing down on him. Then it was Mona's turn. She stood with the same bold confidence she had shown when they first met, introducing herself in a loud fashion.

'Guitar, harmonica, and I sing,' she declared, her voice carrying effortlessly across the hall. But it was the final revelation that left Jake stunned. 'I'm also the soprano at my local opera theatre,' she added casually. Jake's mouth almost hung open in disbelief.

'Thank you Mona,' Professor Baker said. 'Jake Robinson?' She read. Trying not to quiver, Jake stood, all eyes on him. Usually people only looked when he had his violin in hand.

'I'm Jake Robinson. I play the violin and... the piano.' He added, immediately regretting it. He was a novice at best.

'Ah, our residential violinist!' Professor Baker beamed. 'Lovely!'

That's when Jake realised that no one else claimed to play the violin. The trumpet, yes. The keyboard, yes. Even the oboe, but no violin. A quiet sense of reassurance settled over him, and he almost allowed himself to relax. As he was about to sit back down, however, Professor Baker paused, her gaze lingering on him for a moment longer than the others.

'Actually, Jake, I see that you brought your instrument with you. Would you care to play for your fellow classmates?'

At the suggestion, all the eyes around him lit up. They wanted to see him play.

'Go on!' Nudged Mona.

TIMELESS SYMPHONY

Jake nearly stumbled to the front, standing beside the grand piano and his teacher, brandishing his violin. He felt an immense wave of calm, as if cleansing him. When the bow dropped to the strings, Jake played a song that reminded him of his school days. He imagined only Mrs P watching him once again and the melody played with ease as Jake felt the song in his bones. Amongst the notes, somewhere in the far back of his mind, Jake heard a lost promise, one of crafting his own song rather than imitating others and he knew, the next time he played in this hall, in front of people, he would play no other song than one he had crafted himself.

CHAPTER 3
32-33

Thankfully Mona saved the tune, but still, Annabelle sang loud and proud as the pair wished Jake the happiest of birthdays. The cupcake, draped in chocolate icing held a single lit candle. He blew it out with ease.

'What did you wish for?' Mona asked, trying to reach over and dip her finger into the cake.

'No!' Annabelle yelled, silencing Jake. 'You can't tell her, otherwise it won't come true.'

Jake laughed. She said the same thing last year when he had turned thirty-two. 'I think it's obvious what I wished for, don't you?'

As he spoke, Annabelle lifted from her seat, one hand on her hip, trying to poise herself steady. Twinkle had grown quickly in the passing weeks and with each new day, and a heavy groan from Annabelle's tired lips, they inched closer to seeing their baby enter the world. It had been a long, gruelling three years of trying and failing to get pregnant. After the fourth miscarriage, Jake had almost given up hope. He was ready to tell Annabelle that they had to stop trying—that the emotional and physical toll on her was too much to bear. But one morning, at exactly 4 a.m., Annabelle shot out of bed, shouting with excitement.

'I think I'm pregnant!'

She'd had a dream—vivid and strange—where her feet were swollen and she could feel the baby move inside her. Jake, sceptical as ever, thought it was just wishful thinking. She'd had similar dreams before, each one dashed by the painful reality of their struggles. But Annabelle wasn't discouraged. She got up, took a pregnancy test, and as the first light of dawn filled the room, they both watched in stunned silence as the lines appeared, unmistakable and bold. She was pregnant. The joy was immediate, but so was the anxiety. It crept in, quietly at first, then grew more insistent with every passing day. Jake couldn't shake the worry, the fear that something would go wrong again. But then, smoothly, almost imperceptibly, Annabelle entered her second trimester. And with it came a cautious sense of relief.

Jake never thought of himself as a particularly protective man. He had always believed in letting Annabelle move through life as freely as she deserved, without restraints. She still gallivanted, pursued her passions, and did everything she wanted to do, after all, no one argued with Annabelle Robinson. But even so, he found himself watching her more closely than he ever had before. On their evening walks, he made sure to always walk on the side facing oncoming traffic, instinctively positioning himself as her shield. He had no qualms about locking eyes with any man who dared to look at

Annabelle with anything less than respect.

'Hopefully he wished that baby gets your nose rather than his honker.' Mona snorted, picking up the plates to wash. Then ensued the same old argument between the pair. One Annabelle would obviously start by stating that guests aren't supposed to clear the table and Mona reminding her that she hadn't been a guest in over ten years now.

It may have taken two, no five, lectures at university for Jake to warm up to Mona, but it had taken five minutes, no probably two, for Annabelle to adore her. While Jake and Mona's friendship maintained common ground of their shared love of music, it didn't take long for them to share another love: a love of Annabelle.

Too pregnant now to argue, Annabelle relented and resigned herself to the living room and plonked herself on the sofa. In the meantime Mona washed the plates and Jake dutifully dried them.

'You ready for tomorrow?' Mona asked as she unplugged the sink. The water gargling.

'As ready as I'll ever be.'

'He's ready!' Annabelle hollered from the next room.

'He better be!' Mona responded to his wife, snatching the towel from him to dry her wet hands.

As they reconvened in the living room, Jake sat next to Annabelle whose feet were resting on the footstool and her fingers tapped her swollen belly. Mona sat behind the piano and struck a few notes.

'He's going to be great,' Annabelle exhaled. After a long day, she struggled to catch her breath, the baby crushing against Annabelle's ribs.

'It's the big leagues,' Mona continued. 'The Head of Faculty will be there, so you got to be on your A-game.'

Since graduating university with honours, Jake had hoped he could boast about making it big, touring the country, sharing his passion for the violin, and inspiring others to fall in love with its beauty. But the reality was different. He played small gigs in nearby towns, performing at weddings and funerals, rarely making much more than a modest living. His new job was tutoring students at his old school, a role that, at times, felt thankless. He taught kids who were often only there because their parents had pushed them into playing an instrument, making it hard to ignite the same passion in them that he had for music.

'I can't wait to see it,' Annabelle said, closing her heavy eyes. There was a silent, yet loud, glance between Jake and Mona.

You tell her, Jake said with only his eyes.

'Annabelle,' Mona started, catching the cue. 'Are you sure you want to travel all the way to Eldenford? It's a long journey and–'

'And what?' Annabelle bit, trying but failing to sit upright.

'And, well, you're mega-pregnant.'

Jake winced. It wasn't quite the same words Jake used yesterday when he suggested to Annabelle coming wasn't a good idea. Mona continued, 'You of all people should know travelling close to your due date isn't–'

'I want to hear Jake's song.' Annabelle interrupted.

'He can play it for you now,' Mona pointed. 'Can't you Jake?' Ready to grab his instrument from his case, Annabelle clawed his wrist forcing him back to his seat.

'I'm seeing him perform it.'

The argument was futile. When Annabelle made up her mind, that was that. Nothing would change it. So, Jake softly shook his head at Mona and she silenced, returning her attention back to the piano.

It wasn't long after Annabelle announced that she was going to bed. Kissing Jake on the lips and again refusing help when he tried to help her stand.

'I'm pregnant, not legless.'

The pair bid her and Twinkle a good night's sleep, before Jake reached for his cigarettes.

'How's quitting going?' Mona laughed quietly.

'Grand,' he lit the cigarette perched on his lips, before extending the packet to Mona. She took one for herself and together, opening the living room windows, they smoked. From above, Annabelle's congested snoring could be heard.

'I can't believe you're going to be a father,' Mona breathed. 'Are you ready?'

Jake nodded and asked, 'Are you ready to be a god-mother?'

When they had asked Mona to be the baby's god-mother, they had not expected her to cry. In their entire friendship, Jake had never seen Mona cry, not even when she had vomitted on stage during her finals at university which caused her to fail.

'Have you picked a name yet?' Mona asked, flicking the ash into the tray.

'We have one if it's a girl.'

'*Please* tell me it's Mona.'

'Why? Will it make you cry again?'

Mona nudged Jake and the pair chuckled.

'You're going to make a great father, my friend.' Mona exhaled.

'And you'll make a wonderful god-mother,' Jake replied.

The pair sat in a comfortable silence, until their cigarette was smoked and Mona excused herself, saying her farewells. Jake followed the sounds of his snoring wife and prepared for another sleepless night.

The sun stretched itself across her sleeping face. Jake had woken, eaten, showered and dressed, all the while Annabelle remained fast asleep. The rays illuminated her face and her hair sprawled across the pillows. Everybody knows pregnant women glow, but Jake could not imagine anyone radiating such beauty other than his wife. He did not want to disturb, so quietly, he slipped out the bedroom doors.

Mona was awake and sat, crossed legged on the chair, chewing on a piece of toast.

'Morning sunshine,' she smiled.

'Morning,' he replied. 'Are you okay to–'

'Journey with Annabelle to Eldenford?' Mona said, her mouth full. 'Absolutely. I'll get her there.' Jake grabbed his violin case, checking the contents over twice. 'Are you going now?'

He nodded, 'Got a few things to tweak before this evening. Best do it with no distractions.'

'Are you calling me a distraction?' A voice yawned from behind. Annabelle stood in her dressing gown, again holding her bump. Jake knew Annabelle was excited, exhilarated even, to welcome Twinkle into the world but there was also a part of him that knew she would miss being pregnant - despite all its aches and pains.

'The best distraction in the world,' Jake smiled, kissing his wife. She tasted of fresh morning air. 'I can stay if you–'

'Not a chance,' Annabelle replied softly. 'I'll see you there tonight.'

Jake kissed her again, softly this time. Mona was watching and Jake knew he wouldn't leave if he held her for too long. A song awaited him.

Returning to Eldenford always felt strange. Part of him felt as though he had never truly gone to university, while another part couldn't shake the feeling that he had never left. His days at university were spent in the quiet solitude of early mornings, commuting into the city and retreating into practice rooms or sinking into the plush chairs of the library. He'd lose himself for hours in the violin, immersed in books about composers and their complexities. When his classmates returned to their accommodation, Jake waited for the last train home. To them, he was just the musician—an identity he had grown into—but there was another life he led, one that was deeply intertwined with Annabelle. It was the life of managing the endless mortgage left behind by his parents and working as a mechanic on weekends. Despite the weight of it all, the city still captivated him—alive with energy, and holding onto a rustic charm that never lost its pull.

He wandered the Faculty of Music, no longer an undergraduate, but now a guest of honour to play at their summer annual concert. The receptionist pointed to a free practice room.

'Performances aren't until 5pm,' she reminded him.

'Thank you.' Jake smiled, picking up his violin case.

On his way to the room, he recognised no one. Students walked the hallways and Jake wondered if he once looked like them, young and blissful. He couldn't imagine so, until he opened the practice room. It was small, rectangular and familiar. There was a part of him, or maybe his music, that lined the walls.

It felt natural taking out the violin and pulling out the papers of the song he spent the last four years composing and perfecting. In the hours that proceeded, Jake scribbled new notes, pausing, practising and refining.

He practiced relentlessly, the sound of his bow gliding over the strings filling the room until the buzz of people in the adjacent hall filtered through the walls. The crowd was gathering, eager to witness the talent the university showcased, new students and, in his case, an old one. Even as the murmurs and footsteps of the audience echoed outside, Jake kept playing, lost in the music. It wasn't until his phone rang, an unexpected call from the hospital, that he finally stopped.

It was Mona who called, her voice tight with urgency, telling him that Annabelle had gone into labour and that he needed to come back quickly. Jake didn't hesitate. He knew that if Annabelle couldn't witness this performance, no one else would. He didn't bother informing the university of his departure. Instead, he jumped into a taxi, promising the driver triple the fare if he floored it.

An hour and a half later, Jake arrived, breathless and frantic, but it was too late. He was thirteen minutes too late.

It turned out that a lot can happen in thirteen minutes. His wife would bring a baby girl into the world, a healthy 7.5lb baby with all ten fingers and ten toes, her cry a fierce, melodic song. It also turned out that, in thirteen minutes, his wife would suffer with postpartum haemorrhaging. In thirteen minutes, Annabelle Robinson would bring life into this world and die not soon after. And it would be Mona who would choke on her words, telling Jake this in the hallway outside a private room in the labour ward.

'I don't understand,' Jake said, shaking his head. His voice cracking, the words unable to make sense of the nightmare unfolding before him. He watched as Mona collapsed against the hospital wall, her hands tangled in her hair, sobbing uncontrollably. His heart pounded in his chest as he turned and burst into the private room, desperately searching for answers, for something, for anything that made sense.

Two nurses were huddled around a small, *a tiny*, baby bundled in a white blanket. It was the first time Jake ever saw his daughter with her rosy complexion and soft skin.

'Excuse me, sir, you cannot be in here!' A loud voice boomed from behind him. Jake turned to see a surgeon, ungloved and without a cap, approaching with urgency. There were two things Jake remembered vividly about the surgeon: how bright their eyes were, sharp and unyielding, and how vividly red the blood was that splattered across their scrubs, like a horrific, unsettling contrast to the sterile white walls. Then, Jake's gaze shifted to the bed. Annabelle lay there, covered by a blanket up to her bare shoulders, her face as still as the room itself. His breath caught in his throat. He could barely form the words, but somehow, with a voice that matched the surgeon's tone of command, he forced himself to speak.

'I'm the father. I'm her husband.' His voice trembled, though he didn't understand why it seemed so hard to say. It was a nurse who recognised Jake and allowed him to stay. Of course she did. Annabelle worked at the hospital for years.

Jake thought of the early morning where Annabelle slept soundly in their bed and how the warm sun grazed her face. Now, there was only the ugly glow of the orange lamp. She looked small and that's when he thought he would pass out. For there were many words in the English language to describe Annabelle Robinson and small had never been one of them.

'Jake,' a distant voice said. It was the nurse. Her eyes were red. 'Would you like to see your daughter?'

His little girl, the smallest thing he had ever seen, was placed delicately into his arms. Jake wasn't sure how he managed to hold her; he felt like a spirit, caught between this world and the next, suspended in an overwhelming haze. There was nowhere for Jake or his baby girl to sit. He couldn't bring himself to sit on the edge of the hospital bed, terrified that he would disturb Annabelle, as he had that morning when the world still felt whole.

'Annabelle,' Jake whispered.

But she did not move.

'Annabelle,' he said again.

The little girl in his arms stirred. Jake lifted his chin to prevent his tears from staining her untouched skin.

'Annabelle, *please.*' Jake said, looking up at the ceiling. 'You've got to see her.' But Annabelle would not move. She would not twitch herself awake as she did most mornings, turn, yawn and smile. She would not say good morning. She would not purr the name *Jakey* from her sleepy mouth. She would not whisper the name of their daughter, as he had imagined. It would be later when Jake would discover, in a hushed, grief-stricken moment with the nurse, that Annabelle's dying words had been their daughter's name.

'Harriet.'

Somehow Jake willed himself to look at his unmoving wife, and it was then when Harriet started to cry. Maybe it was his daughter's way of telling her father it was okay to be sad, because when her cries filled the air, so did Jake's.

Jake knew how to do many things. He knew how to smooth bow his violin, tenuto too. He knew how to replace an engine on almost any car. He knew that there were exactly fifty-one steps from his old childhood bedroom to the garage - something he discovered as a child. But there were two things he did not know how to do: raise a child or exist in a world without Annabelle.

Yet there he was, walking into an empty home, Harriet in her bassinet surrounded only by the reminders of Annabelle's existence. Her slippers that sat by the stairs; her books on pregnancy and gardening, gifted by her mother; her favoured blanket that she always huddled into after a particularly long and strenuous shift at the hospital.

'Let me help,' Mona offered, stumbling into the house after Jake. She carried the bag Annabelle meticulously packed for the birth. Mona saw him staring at the bag, said nothing, and lowered it to the ground by Harriet who remained sleeping. Harriet who would never know a life with Annabelle.

'I'll make a cup of tea—'

'No.' Jake's voice trembled. 'No.'

Jake didn't know if it was Annabelle or Mona who last made tea in their house, but Jake feared to touch any item that was last held by Annabelle's fingertips.

'I'll make it.' Jake said. 'Could you put Harriet in her cot?'

Mona nodded and took Jake's daughter upstairs. Jake floated through the house, his feet not belonging to him, but then again, Jake had never belonged to himself. He had been his parents, and then just his father's and, always, Annabelle's. He belonged to no one other than Annabelle but was now forced to exist in a reality where she did not.

Jake did not hear Mona creep behind him. He did not know she watched as Jake fell onto the dining chair, grasping at the edges of the table, sobbing. Not until she wrapped her arms around him and together, they cried.

Later, Mona would make him a cup of tea. One he would not drink. Instead, he would stay up smoking, feeding Harriet baby formula in intervals and, in the forsaken hours in the morning, fall into a restless sleep.

'You can't bring a baby to a funeral!' Mona said, burping Harriet.

Before Annabelle's passing, Mona frequently stayed over, sleeping on the sofa before returning home up north. Now, she was a part of the furniture - the sofa in fact. She lived out of a small, rather pathetic, backpack and often wore the same clothes on rotation. Washing her items along with Jake's and Harriet's.

'Well, what do you suggest?' Jake asked, blowing the last of his cigarette smoke outside and closing the door behind him. He made his feelings about a babysitter abundantly clear. At two weeks old, no one but him and Mona looked after her.

'I don't know.' Mona whined. The pitch irritated Jake. 'But

bringing a baby into an environment surrounded by so much grief seems… wrong.'

'Mona.' Jake's voice hardened. 'It's all she's ever known.'

He was right. Despite their efforts, blowing bubbles and kissing her round belly, Harriet was born into grief.

Mona shook her head. 'No, that is not true.'

It was later when Harriet was asleep in her cot and Jake hung up the phone on the funeral directors, finalising plans for tomorrow, lighting yet another cigarette, Mona came down the stairs with a baby blanket thrown over her shoulder, and said,

'Fine, but she's not wearing black.'

Jake agreed.

'We can put her in yellow, or blue or–'

'Violet.' Jake interrupted. It was from the shadows, many years ago, an angel emerged into Jake's life wearing a violet dress and puffing on a cigarette. Mona was not privy to this memory, but she knew whatever it was that had Jake smile gently was not to be disagreed with.

'Violet it is.'

Jake did not think he was capable. Standing in front of a church, full of people who held onto their tissues, weeping, but he knew that this moment was bigger, more important than himself.

He could not look at Mona who cried into a tissue or Harriet who slept in her arms. He could not bear witness to Annabelle's parents who never thought they'd outlive their daughter. Jake averted his eyes from Anje, the nurse who had delivered Harriet and placed her into his arms, or Mrs P, who sobbed silently on the back pew. He ignored Marco, Lottie and Ritchie. He couldn't even face their local grocer who helped Annabelle pack her food when she was too heavily pregnant.

Jake's eyes rested on the coffin he helped carry to the front, still unable to comprehend that Annabelle was inside. For if it were up to him, he would crawl in, lie with her and be buried beneath the earth. It was Harriet's gentle stir that reminded him why he stayed.

Somehow, standing at the front, Jake spoke. His voice cracked at first, but as the words tumbled out, he recalled moments of Annabelle with a clarity that nearly stopped his heart. He remembered her running towards him at the beach on their third anniversary, her laughter carrying through the wind as she tripped and fell into a child's sandcastle, destroying it completely. Jake's breath hitched as he smiled, and he could almost hear the laughter ripple through the church, as the memory of Annabelle's infectious energy filled the room. The whole congregation chuckled, recalling how, instead of walking away in embarrassment, Annabelle had spent the next hour rebuilding the sandcastle with the child, teaching them how to do it better.

And that's when he cried.

For Annabelle Robinson had been both soft and hard, kind and stern, loud but seldom quiet. She was the type of woman who could light up a room with her smile, but whose resolve could tear down walls when needed. Her energy – that fire, that warmth, that unstoppable force – washed over him, and Jake's chest tightened. He wept not just for the woman she was, but for the world that would never feel her presence in the same way again. And he knew that whatever force had taken her from him would have to face her wrath – a wrath unlike any other.

But in that grief, there was a flicker of clarity. He had a daughter now, a daughter who needed him as much as he needed her. Jake steadied himself, knowing Annabelle would trust him to raise Harriet with all the love and grace he could muster, even though he had no idea how. He would be a good father, for Annabelle, for Harriet. He'd figure it out. And Annabelle would be thankful. She would be thankful for Mona, especially, who would be there every step of the way, offering her time, her love, and her unwavering support to raise Harriet. Together, they would make sure their daughter knew how much she was loved, how much her mother had loved her, even from the very beginning.

After the service, during the wake, for the first time ever in Jake's life, he considered ordering a glass of whiskey. It was also the first time Jake understood why his father had drank himself into an early grave. However, Jake was not his father, and instead of holding a bottle that night, he held his daughter.

He barely read the letter at first. He recognised the stamp, he even recognised the handwriting, but when he ripped the envelope open, in the middle of trying to stop Harriet crying, Jake thought nothing of it. It meant little when Eldenford informed him that his opportunity to perform for the Head Faculty of Music had been missed – and another would not be presenting itself any time soon. But when he picked it up for the second time, the ache in his feet throbbing and the bags under his eyes weighing him down, it compelled him to pause, to take in his surroundings, and to confront the reality of what he needed to do.

'Don't be ridiculous!' Mona scoffed, shaking her head. 'You can't give up.'

Jake shook his head. 'I'm not giving up.' At least he didn't think he was. 'I just gotta be realistic about this, Mona. I mean, tutoring won't carry us through.'

Mona disagreed, and she made her opinion known. She said they would figure it out, somehow, that putting the violin down wasn't necessary, but it was early when Jake called Ritchie asking him if he would let Jake work at the garage again.

'Are you sure Jake?' Ritchie yawned. Jake had woken him up, the birds weren't even singing yet.

'Yes, I'm sure.'

'Okay, I'll ask Stevie to put you back on payroll. When do you want to start?'

Jake stared into the dusty, desolate attic. The large chest was open and in it lay his violin and all the songs he would never play again.

'Today.' Jake said, shutting the trunk.

CHAPTER 4
43-44

'Again.' Jake said, not even looking at her. He tilted his pencil and started shading. A heavy whine echoed in the background. 'I said, *again*.' He did not raise his voice, but the command was followed and the room flooded with the sweet melody from the piano. It occupied all the spaces of the empty room only, however, for fifty seconds before the wrong chord interrupted the tune.

'Shit!' she cursed.

'Oi,' Jake bit, glancing his eyes up through his specs.

'Sorry,' Harriet said quietly. 'I didn't mean to–'

'Again.'

'Nooo!' She stood from the stool. 'I'm tired of getting it wrong.'

'So, play it right.' Jake smiled, putting the pencil down.

'Very funny, Dad.' Harriet huffed, plonking back down. The young girl tugged at her sleeves, preventing her fingers from playing another note. Jake took this opportunity to intervene. He sat behind the piano and beckoned his daughter to perch beside him. He struck the first three keys.

'Play with your frustration rather than against it.'

'I don't even know what that means.' She rolled her eyes.

There had been countless moments when Jake nearly called Harriet Annabelle. Though she looked every bit like him, with her murky grey eyes and thin lips, her attitude was unmistakably her mother's.

'It means you lean into the instrument.' Again, the words were lost on her. 'If you don't want to play then–'

'No!' Harriet interjected. The question worked like a charm every time, she was far too stubborn to give up. She rolled up her sleeves and Jake did not leave her side. Instead he watched as she closed her eyes and played the entire song.

Some time, during her solo performance, the postman had been and gone. In his wake he left a series of white envelopes, one larger than the rest that Jake immediately recognised.

'Take a break,' Jake said to Harriet, eyeing the stamp. Harriet jumped from the piano and dashed upstairs to her room. A loud slam followed. He dreaded the years to come - the teen era. But today brought a new dilemma. One that had many numbers behind the pound sign.

This time, it was Jake's turn to curse. The academy was both prestigious and promising, offering Harriet musical opportunities that Jake could only have dreamed of as a child. But like everything in life, it came with a price—one that Jake's unrelenting shifts as a mechanic could never satisfy. The letter before him, sprawled across the dining room table, forced him to confront the harsh truth: not even hard work could make up for what was missing. The day had finally come.

The phone rang and from above a door swung open, followed by a series of, 'I'll get it! I'll get it!' Harriet raced to answer the phone on the wall, running past Jake so fast she created a rush of wind. He could only raise an eyebrow as he watched Harriet's face fall as she answered.

'Oh hi.' She extended the receiver to her father. 'It's Auntie Mona.'

'Expecting someone else were you?' He smirked. His daughter blushed as he put the phone to his ear. 'Hi Mona.'

'Tell her she's an ungrateful runt, will you?' Mona breathed.

'Auntie Mona says she loves you!' Jake called, but he was only met with the slamming of her bedroom door. 'She said I love you back.'

'You're a terrible liar, you know that?'

'What do you want Mona?' Jake held the letter up, tilting it against the light, hoping the number had miraculously reduced.

'Just checking if you are still coming tonight.'
Two tickets were pinned on the calendar for Mona's performance tonight.

'Yep, we're coming.'

'Good, good. What time will you arrive at the station?'
But Jake was not listening when he replied,

'Hmmhmm, all good.'

'What's going on with you?' Mona asked. 'Not having a

stroke are you?'

'Nearly.' And that's when he told her: the day had come. The day he had to sell his father's 1951 Vincent Black Lightning. If Annabelle were here, she would have come up with a thousand alternative solutions, anything to avoid selling the bike. She understood what it meant to him, what it had meant to his father. But Mona, without missing a beat, exhaled sharply and muttered,

'Oh, that sucks.'

'It does.' Jake replied, the weight of it settling in.
Jake still yearned for Annabelle. There was an ache inside of him, deep and persistent, that would never truly disappear. It had settled into him like an old, familiar wound, always there, a constant presence. Over time, the ache had become malleable, something he could shape smaller when necessary, like when Harriet needed him, or on days like her birthday. The day was a delicate balance, entwining both the joy of watching his daughter grow and the grief that lingered in his chest.

'You gotta do what you gotta do.' Mona said, reminding Jake of his priorities. She asked him important questions like, 'Who are you going to sell it to?'

There were many collectors across the country who were burning to buy that bike, Jake knew that. They contacted him often to see if a new, bigger figure could change his mind.

'I'll find someone.' Jake said. It was the sound of a melody that distracted him. He told Mona he'd see her later and tucked the envelope in his back pocket. When he walked back into the living room, he saw Harriet sat behind the piano, practising. He'd sell it all if it meant hearing her play.

As the train rocked, Harriet's head was deep in a book. Jake occasionally glanced out the window, before opening his sketchpad and continuing his drawing. Out of her world of fictional characters, Harriet looked over her father's arm.

'Was she really that pretty?'

Jake started drawing shortly after Annabelle's death. It began with her eyes, the way they glistened, especially in the sunlight, like amber liquid caught in a fleeting moment. He never wanted to forget that sparkle, the way they shone when she smiled or when she looked at him with a kind of understanding only she could offer. But as he tried to capture that light on paper, frustration set in. His hands couldn't replicate the warmth and depth of her gaze. The more he drew, the more obsessed he became with perfecting every detail, as though each stroke could bring her back, or at least make her real again. Soon, he focused on her lips, soft and inviting, the way they curled when she laughed or whispered his name. Then, it was her hands, delicate and expressive, the way they held his or gently tucked a strand of hair behind her ear. And then, her face, those little imperfections that had made her uniquely hers. But no matter how hard he tried, no matter how many sketches he did, he could never capture her the way she deserved. Yet, he couldn't stop. Drawing her was the closest he came to holding her again. It was the only way he could feel her near, other than hugging Harriet, who, like her mother, had eyes that glistened in the sun, though in a way that was uniquely her own.

'She was prettier.' Jake said.

He never cried about Annabelle in front of Harriet. He spoke only when he felt confident, when he knew his voice wouldn't break. Harriet deserved to think of her mother only as a shining light, not the shadows she left behind after her death.

Harriet took the pad from her father's grip and her index finger traced along her mother's cheek.

'Did I ever tell you about the time your mother scared off my school bullies?' Jake asked, despite knowing he had told her the story countless times. Like always, Harriet listened. Jake always assumed Harriet wanted to hear stories of her mother, but the truth was Harriet listened so she could see her father smile. She was convinced the only time she ever saw her father truly happy was when he spoke of her mother. So, she let him tell her stories she heard time and time again, and let him live in a kinder world - one where had both a wife and daughter.

'Auntie Mona will meet us at the theatre.' Jake said, holding his daughter's hand, refusing to let go amongst the chaos of London's bustling streets.

'You went to school near here right?' Harriet asked, looking around at the towering buildings, happy to let her father direct them through the herds of people.

'University,' he corrected. 'Close, about an hour away.'

Jake hadn't thought of Eldenford in a long time. He had to choose what occupied his mind. Eldenford had its own individual, heavy weight. One that Jake could not bear, not along with everything else.

'So, I was thinking–' Jake smiled, '–that tonight we'd have popcorn for dinner.'

Harriet's face lit up. 'And coke?'

'Absolutely, kiddo.' He laughed.

Jake had always imagined his life playing out differently. He thought he'd spend more of it on a stage in a tux, violin in hand, than beneath a jacked-up car, stained in oil and grease. But life, as it often does, had dealt him a different hand. And so, here he was, in the darkness of a theatre, watching as the curtains parted and revealed Mona, standing alone on the raised platform. She sang with a depth and richness in her voice that reached new heights, notes she had spent years perfecting, both in the practice rooms at Eldenford and in their living room, where Annabelle would ask her to sing for them. In those early years, after Annabelle's death, Mona had sung for Harriet. No pacifier or toy could calm the baby's cries; only Mona's voice, warm and gentle, could soothe her. Now, Harriet's response to Mona's singing had shifted. Where once it lulled her to sleep, now it held her rapt, her eyes wide, glistening with emotion, as she watched her aunt command the stage with an intensity that held the entire audience in thrall.

Gone was the punk rocker look that had once defined Mona; in its place stood a woman of grace and elegance. She wore a silky black evening dress that caught the light with every subtle movement, and long gold earrings that framed her face, accentuating the sleek, straight black hair now touched with strands of silver. Even the tattoos that marked her were hidden beneath layers of thick makeup. From the third row, it was impossible to see the faded ink of a past mistake.

The standing ovation Mona received was well-deserved. Jake clapped loud and when that was not enough, he put two fingers in his mouth and whistled. Mona's eyes instantly fell on his but when they met Harriet's, tears swelled in the singer's eyes. With no decorum, she waved and stuck her tongue out at Harriet.

'Can we go and see her backstage?' Harriet asked as everyone continued to clap.

'Let's go!' Jake said, his voice eager. But as he turned to lead Harriet out, something made him pause. At the back of the theatre, a woman stood, her figure outlined by the dim glow of the exit lights. She wore a slender dress that draped elegantly around her, and her short blonde bob framed her face with a softness that made his chest tighten. Jake's breath caught in his throat, his heart skipping a beat as he tried to clear the fog in his vision, still thick with the emotion of Mona's performance. He blinked hard, focusing through the blur of tears, and the woman remained there, unmoving, like a vision pulled from a distant memory. His chest constricted again, but this time, the ache wasn't quite as sharp. He looked again, breathing easier as his mind shifted back to reality. She was just a woman, standing quietly in the shadows, no one he knew.

'Dad?' Harriet said, trying to push him.

Jake did not look behind again.

The night air was cool as the three of them stepped out of the restaurant, the streets around them quieter than before. Their evening had been filled with heavy carbs, ice-creamed induced laughter, and stories that seemed to stretch on forever. Harriet's joy was infectious, her giggles bubbling up like music whenever Mona was near. She whispered secrets into Mona's ear, secrets that Jake was never meant to hear, as they walked towards Mona's apartment.

Later, once Harriet had drifted off to sleep in the spare room, Mona leaned back, a teasing smile curling on her lips.

'She has a crush,' Mona revealed with a chuckle, her eyes

sparkling with mischief. Jake's eyebrows lifted, the tiniest flicker of surprise crossing his face.

'A crush?' he repeated, amused and curious.

'Oh yes,' Mona continued, her voice lower now, 'A boy in her class. She's got it bad.'

'I should've guessed.' Jake replied as Mona perched on the armrest.

'A drummer in her class.'

Jake groaned, 'A drummer?'

'What would you'd rather?' Mona laughed. 'A harmonica player?'

'No, I've heard people that play the harmonica are crazy.' He smiled, and Mona nudged him gently. 'No, I would rather her love be for her own instrument.'

Mona scoffed, a sharp sound cutting through the air. 'That's hypocritical.'

Jake's gaze hardened, his eyes narrowing slightly, but Mona didn't flinch. She held his stare with an intensity that made him uncomfortable. She always did this—always poked at him when it came to the violin. Mona didn't let things slide, and the violin was a topic she never let go of, even when Jake asked her, more than once, to steer clear of it.

'I guess I deserved that,' Jake muttered, shrugging his shoulders in resignation. His voice was quieter now as he leaned back against the worn armrest.

Mona agreed and excused herself to fetch them a few

drinks as Jake attempted to plump his cushions for the night. The apartment was luxurious, adorned with high ceilings and large open windows that overlooked central London. On the walls were various photos of Mona on stage. She did not shy away from her success - the unlikely northern orphan who bounced from school-to-school, now performing on stages people dreamed of.

Mona passed Jake his glass of icy water and held tightly onto her nightcap of red wine. She wedged herself beside Jake, sighing and pulling out a packet of cigarettes that was wedged in the cracks of the sofa.

'For old times' sake?'

Harriet begged Jake to stop smoking, her voice always laced with concern, and for a while, he tried. He fought the cravings, during his morning coffee, the long hours at work, and especially that one cigarette before bed, the ritual he'd always cherished. But one evening, as he flipped through a box of old memories, he came across a photo booth strip of him and Annabelle. The pictures captured moments of their carefree laughter, their playful faces, and then, two frames showing them locked in a kiss. They hadn't even noticed the camera had clicked the fourth time, lost in the moment, as they always had been. Jake took a cigarette from the packet and lit it.

Into the silent room, with her face clouded by smoke, Mona said,

'I love you, Jake.'

He blinked at her a few times until he softened and smiled.

'I love you too, Mona.'

Because he did. He loved her and all she had done and sacrificed to help him become the father he was today. God knows, she could've been performing in London years before she had made it, if she wasn't living out of a backpack and burping Harriet late at night.

Jake did not expect Mona's lips to fall on his. One hand holding her cigarette, the other still grasping the neck of her wine glass. Jake returned the kiss. The moment made his skin flush, but it was him who pulled away first.

People often asked him when he would move on, when he would start dating again. Even Annabelle's parents, before they passed, had encouraged him to find someone new. And while Jake certainly felt the pull of lust and desire, he knew that before he was a man with urges, he was Annabelle's. Trying to pretend otherwise would be nothing but a betrayal of everything they had shared.

Mona was striking, impossible to ignore, with a presence that could fill a room. And Jake couldn't help but acknowledge how time had passed. He and Mona had moved from their twenties into their thirties, and ultimately into their forties. Mona, who had joined Eldenford at eighteen, had grown into a woman of incredible depth and strength, and Jake realised, with a slight pang, that they had slipped into middle age almost without noticing. The wrinkles, the greying hair, the specs he never imagined he'd wear, they were all symbols of time, but Jake had never truly witnessed their aging. What he felt instead was their growth, the shared evolution of two people who had weathered so much together.

And even though Jake knew, deep down, that Annabelle would have wanted him to find happiness again, especially with someone like Mona, he couldn't bring himself to move on. In his heart, he would always be Annabelle's.

'Mona.'

'I know.' Her eyes were closed when she smiled. 'I just had to see.'

He was glad she had, because, although he never admitted it out loud, he too had wondered. The thought first blossomed in him years ago, when he had watched Mona return home from a date, standing on his doorstep, kissing someone passionately goodnight. He had watched from his bedroom window, the image searing into his mind as he lay awake that night, wondering what it would be like to kiss her.

Now that he had, he knew he never wanted to again. There was no regret, no longing, just a quiet certainty that settled deep within him. He realised the lips he desired, the ones that had once teased his thoughts, would only ever live now in the soft strokes of his pencil on paper.

'I thought I saw her today,' Mona mumbled, her lips now against her glass. The red liquid staining her tongue. The revelation nearly made Jake jolt, but he remained still. He did not tell Mona he too had a similar experience.

'It freaked me the fuck out,' she added, downing her drink all in one. 'Then I realised how ludicrous it was. If Annabelle was anywhere, she would never leave your damn side, that's for sure.'

It made Jake laugh, and at some point during the night, after hours of talking, the pair fell asleep. Mona's head on Jake's shoulder. His hand resting on top of hers.

'Brilliant.' Jake said, gently clapping. 'That'll blow the absolute socks off of them.'

Harriet's smile almost touched her ears, 'Yeah? Are you sure?'

'I'm sure.' Jake replied, but Harriet still pressed on.

'Do you think–'

There was a heavy knock at the door. Harriet looked at her father expectedly, but he told her to practise again.

'It's just a mechanic from the garage grabbing a part he needs.' Jake grabbed the keys off the hook. 'I'll be back in a sec.'

Dutifully, Harriet's attention returned back to the piano, while Jake shook the large man's hand, feeling the roughness of his calloused grip, before guiding him into the garage. The air inside was thick with the scent of oil and metal. It didn't take long, just a few swift movements, before Jake whipped the cover from the bike and turned on the engine, the familiar rumble filling the space. The man, eyes gleaming with satisfaction, produced a cheque from his jacket pocket. Jake thought it would be harder, the moment he'd feared for so long, giving him the keys. But they slipped from his fingers, almost without his consent, falling into the man's open palm.

'I'll drop off the ownership papers once the cheque has cleared.' Jake said.

The man barely listened as he caressed the metal. There was one thing Jake couldn't do and that was watch as the bike was wheeled out of the garage.

The bike was never mentioned again. No one asked about it. No one knew. The money paid for Harriet's tuition until she graduated. It was only later - *a lot later* - when Harriet was old and greying herself when she wondered how her father, a simple mechanic, had seen her through such an expensive academy. Until then, Jake avoided the garage at all costs. The remnants of his father's presence now gone.

It was a random Tuesday when Jake returned home from work, fingers stained with muck and grease when he saw Harriet curled up on the sofa reading a book.

'What you got there?' Jake asked, pulling his boots off.

'We had to pair up with another student and learn about their instrument and pick a book on one of their favourite composers.'

'Not the drums, is it?' Jake eyed and that's when he saw the front page. It was a book on Pierre Rode. It wasn't his copy. His was old, withered by years of use. It was also hidden away, tucked up in a box in the attic.

'What? No. It's the violin.' Harriet eyed him back. 'But I have to read *all of this* before I'm even allowed to hold it. Teacher's rules.' Harriet sighed, reopening the book. 'Which I will because do you know how cool violinists are?'

Jake had to hide his smirk. He never told Harriet about his violin days. It was long ago now, forgotten.

'They're cool, are they?' Jake asked, walking into the kitchen ready to make them dinner. He couldn't help but laugh when a sudden cough caught him by surprise. He tried to clear his chest but it caught in his throat and it took a few seconds to catch his breath. From the other room, Harriet told him to get a drink of water. Jake stifled it, wiping a tear that threatened to fall from his eyelash. When he could, he took a deep breath of air.

CHAPTER 5
54-55

You always want someone by your side when good things happen, bad too. What you don't realise is sometimes you need someone. Jake found that out when he sat on the hard, blue plastic chair opposite the man who held onto a folder, for Jake had no idea what was happening and he had no one to relay it back to him. No one to tell him what was going on when the doctor said,

'It is treatable, but only if you start the treatment as soon as possible.'

'Right.' Jake said. The hospital's windows were wide open and depicted the scene of a quiet, green garden. There were no birds in the sky.

'When?' Jake said, shaking his head trying to stay in the room.

'Tomorrow.'

'Tomorrow?' Jake repeated, nearly laughing. 'But my shift is at—' The look in the doctor's eyes silenced him. 'Okay, tomorrow. When do you think–' He was interrupted by a sudden, yet familiar, cough. It took him even longer than usual to catch his breath. The doctor quietly gave him a tissue and when he spotted the crimson red soaking itself into the white, he said

'Tomorrow, Mr Robinson. Your treatment starts

tomorrow.'

On the way home, Jake pulled over on the side of the road trying to catch his breath yet again. The gasp of air afterwards was always bittersweet. The oxygen returning to his lungs was a relief, but it never felt like enough. He needed more.

As he stood up straight, Jake's eyes scanned through the thick trees, the light filtering through the leaves to reveal a familiar lake nestled just beyond the branches. The sun dappled the ground in patches, casting a gentle warmth across Jake's skin. He had nowhere to be. Harriet wouldn't be home for hours, and he wasn't due to work until later, so locking his car, Jake moved forward, his boots crunching lightly on the gravel path. The air felt heavy with quiet, the kind that only a place like this could offer, and it pulled him in. With each step, he felt his chest tighten slightly, not from the usual cough that had become more frequent, but from something deeper, something he couldn't quite name. The lake ahead looked just as it always had — tranquil, serene. A rush of emotion caught him by surprise, the kind that felt like an old wound being reopened. Jake stood at the edge of the lake, his eyes traced the familiar outline of the water, the same lake where Annabelle had come home after returning from university. Jake stood there for who knows how long, closing his eyes, trying to remember the softness of her hands.

'Winston!' A loud voice called and galloping from the trees

came a large shaggy dog. It dashed straight between Jake's legs, almost knocking him off balance. He stumbled but caught himself, chuckling as the dog circled back, its tail wagging furiously in excitement.

'I'm so sorry!' A young woman winced as she approached, demanding Winston to sit.

'It's okay.' Jake stroked his fur. 'Wow, he's a big dog.'

'Yeah, and a big pain in the arse.' She clipped the dog's lead back on. The woman stared at Jake, her eyes deep in study, before clicking her fingers. 'Hey, I know you!'

She was young, probably Harriet's age, if not younger.

'You're Mr Robinson. Harriet's dad?'

Jake nodded.

'I'm Laura.' The name didn't ring a bell. 'Lottie Mansfield's daughter?' The revelation made Jake's eyes pop wide.

'Wow, look at you. I haven't seen you since you were, what, three?'

Harriet was five when she was invited to Laura's birthday party. There had been a bouncy castle and lots of cake. It felt like yesterday when Jake watched Harriet jump as high as she could to catch the bubbles that blew around the garden while all the other kids begged for another slice of that cake.

'How's your mother?' Jake asked absentmindedly.

He hadn't seen Lottie since the party. Even with children, they had little in common anymore. Their friendship had always been tethered to Annabelle, and when she passed, so did the reason to keep in touch.

'Good, good.' Laura smiled. She looked exactly like her mother had done in her teens. 'I'll tell her you said hello.'
The conversation lost momentum and Laura said her goodbyes, tugging at Winston's leash to follow. 'You look well Mr Robinson.'

Jake found the comment amusing.
He stayed at the lake a moment longer, looking down at the algae infested waters.

'Give me strength,' he whispered. His words were swept away by the wind, and in that moment, he silently prayed that wherever Annabelle was, she would guide him through the thing he had to do, yet feared more than anything.

In simple words, he bottled it. Harriet's visit was fleeting. She came home and started faffing in her wardrobe, pulling clothes from the hanger, snapping the plastic in two. She had a party at her friend's, one with promises of free food and musicians showcasing their talent.

'I was thinking of playing the violin because we have like five piano players.' She explained, putting on a denim jacket. Jake hovered under the doorway for too long. 'Dad? Are you okay?'

'Oh, I'm fine.' He smiled.

'Would you rather I stayed?'

Harriet spent many evenings with her old man, even when it

was considered the 'uncool' thing to do.

'Don't be so silly,' Jake said. 'I'll be up when you're home.' They both knew it wasn't true. He'd be asleep, potentially on the sofa, potentially in his bed. Harriet gave him a kiss when she left and told him she loved him.

'I love you too.'

But she was already out the door.

Left in the house alone, Jake paced past the phone a few times. He stopped every so often and pondered his decision. Punching the numbers in felt wrong and when it dialled twice, he hung up. Seconds later, it rang.

'Why did you hang up?' Mona asked. 'I was just about to pick up!'

'I…' Jake faltered.

With a gentle nudge, Mona asked him what was wrong, so he told her. He told her everything he could remember from the appointment, though in truth, it wasn't much. The details felt scattered, like pieces of a puzzle he couldn't quite fit together, but he spoke them all the same.

'You have cancer?'

The doctor had said the word calmly, almost pragmatically. Mona repeated it in a way that made Jake's heart ache as much as his lungs.

'Have you told Harriet yet?'

'I'm not telling her.'

'You're what?' Mona's hard edge returned. 'Don't be so

ridiculous.'

'It's not ridiculous.' Jake stiffened.

'Yes, it fucking is.' Mona snapped. 'You're having treatment tomorrow and you're not going to tell her?'

Jake had nearly forgotten he relayed that detail.

'You need to tell her.'

'Stop it Mona.'

'No! Jake you have to–'

'I said stop it!' Jake yelled. Of course, the sudden increase in volume made his chest tighten. The pressure built up, and before he could steady himself, a cough escaped, jagged and forceful. He fumbled to hang up the phone, his breathing laboured, as the coughs racked his body, each one deeper and more relentless than the last.

The tea soothed his aching throat. He sat at the head of the empty table and stared into the amber liquid. Maybe Mona was right. How would he hide this from Harriet? She was the one who had pestered him for years, nagging him to book an appointment ever since the cough first started. A cough he tried to ignore, hoping it would fade. But eventually, he gave in and booked the appointment, doing it in secret.

The front door gently creaked open and Jake looked at his watch that read 9pm.

'Gee, this is early by your standards. Was the party really that bad? Didn't get stage fright, I hope!'

Jake did not expect to see Mona trail into the kitchen, red faced with Harriet in her hand.

'Is it true?' His daughter choked with tears streaming down her face.

The urge to kick Mona out of his house, out of his life, surged from deep within Jake. She had overstepped her bounds, betrayed his trust. He had always prided himself on having the final say when it came to Harriet; after all, he was the parent. But as Harriet gripped Mona's palm, he realised with a heavy heart that it wasn't that simple. Mona's influence on Harriet was just as vital as his own.

'It's true.' Jake said, rising from his seat.

Harriet flung herself into Jake's arms. She clawed his back and held him so tight it was as though she was trying to anchor him to this earth for eternity. From over Harriet's shoulder, Mona mouthed,

I'm sorry. She too was crying. *I had to.*

Jake gently stoked Harriet's long hair.

Thank you. He mouthed back.

Mona had done what needed to be done, of what he was too afraid to do. Mona slipped out of the room as Jake continued to hold Harriet.

'Dad,' Harriet sobbed. 'You can't leave me. Please don't leave me.'

Jake knew he shouldn't make promises he couldn't keep, but still the words fell from his lips,

'I won't darling. I'm not going anywhere.'

For the first time since the news, Jake cried.

Once upon a time, he would've carried her to bed. He would've lifted his little girl in his arms, trailed upstairs and tucked her into bed. But Harriet was no longer a little girl, but a woman. A woman who was curled on the sofa, wrapped in a bundle of blankets. Jake realised there must have been a day when he lowered Harriet from his arms and never picked her up again. He wished he could pinpoint when, but it evaded him entirely. Mona sat on the piano stool but the instrument lid was closed. She too stared at Harriet. The clock ticked into the early hours of the morning.

'Mona,' Jake said quietly. 'You have to promise me–'

'I swear to God–' Mona whispered through gritted teeth. 'If you say anything stupid right now, I will hit you.' Mona finally looked him in the eye, tears threatening to fall from her lashes. 'Don't you dare.'

'Okay.' He relaxed into the sofa.

'You're going to get treatment and you're going to be fine.' Mona continued.

'Okay.'

'No.' Mona bit. 'Tell me.'

'I'm going to get treatment.' Jake conceded.

'And…?'

Jake remained silent. The words were nowhere near his lips.

Mona lifted from her seat and knelt in front of Jake. Her cold hands enclosed around his.

'I'm not saying this for me, Jake.'

The comment made him lightly chuckle.

'Okay, fine, maybe it's for me a little bit.' She smiled but it didn't reach her eyes. 'But I'm serious. You need to believe it too. You need to believe that you will be okay.'

That's when Jake realised how ridiculous it would have been to ask Mona to promise to look after Harriet if the worst were to happen. She didn't need to say the words; it was already understood between them.

'It'll be okay,' Jake replied, stroking Mona's hand. 'It'll all be okay.'

'I'm sorry, Mr Robinson.' The receptionist said as Harriet clung onto Jake's hand.

'That is totally unacceptable.' Mona said. 'His consultant explicitly said his treatment would be immediate. Look!' Mona said, grabbing the paper and waving it in the air.

'I appreciate your frustration, Mrs Robinson, however the consultant needs to review his notes and the appointment will be rescheduled for tomorrow.'

No one corrected the mistake. Instead, Mona leant into the role of belligerent spouse that Jake imagined Annabelle doing. Upon feeling Harriet's fingers quiver, Jake eventually pulled Mona away, informing the receptionist he would await his consultant's phone call and be back tomorrow.

From the building to the car, Mona swore, loudly and with no apology, her voice sharp and cutting through the tense air. She paced ahead, clearly frustrated, the clicking of her heels against the pavement matching the fast rhythm of her thoughts.

'I can drive,' Harriet offered quietly, but Jake declined and set off, the weight of the day pulling at him. He gripped the steering wheel with firm, deliberate hands, needing to focus on the simple, grounding task of driving to keep his mind from wandering too far into places he wasn't ready to go.

They drove in silence. Jake stifled his cough until it erupted from his chest and he pulled his handkerchief out. Harriet, in his back mirror, winced and Mona only stared when she saw the blood. Even with the window open, the car felt stagnant, heavy. That's when he decided to miss the exit.

'Hey,' Mona said without missing a beat. 'Where are you going?' She pointed at the junction.

'Just trust me.' Jake said.

By the hour mark, the pair started to moan. Harriet needed the bathroom. Mona wanted a coffee. Jake laughed when they begged him to reveal the destination, but silence followed when the coast came into view.

There were no clouds in the sky, but the wind was strong, tugging at their clothes as they parked and stepped out onto the empty beach. The sun hung high, casting a warm golden glow that made the water shimmer, its surface dancing with sunlight as the waves rolled in, foaming white and breaking against the shore in a rhythmic lullaby. The air smelled salty, fresh, and alive.

There was an unspoken magic between them when the three of them kicked off their shoes and socks, and their toes sank into the sand. Mona wasted no time and made her way to the kiosk to buy a coffee, leaving Jake and Harriet to stroll along the water's edge; the wet sand cool against their bare feet as they wandered slowly. The only sound was the gentle roar of the ocean, the distant call of seagulls, and the soft crunch of their footsteps in the sand.

'You know this place stole your mother from me for three years.' He smiled.

'Ah, I forgot she attended university here.'

'It was only a matter of time before she came home.'

Harriet plodded her feet into the water and squealed as the low temperature hit her skin. The laughter that followed was hearty and full. Jake wished he could bottle that sound and keep it in his pocket.

'OI!' A voice yelled. Mona, finishing the last of her coffee, plonked the cup into the sand and started viciously tugging at her clothes.

'She's not… is she?' Harriet asked, but it was too late. In only her underwear, Mona ran into the sea, crashing against a wave, screeching with glee.

'C'MON!'

'Oh, what the hell.' Jake laughed as Mona dove beneath the water. He pulled at his clothes, right down to his boxers, flinging his jeans and jumper safely away from the water's reach. Then, he ran.

The water collided against his skin. The cold made him gasp, but he did not cough. Instead, he pushed his head under and the salty water glided across his cheeks. As he met with Mona in the depths, she splashed him.

'It's fucking freezing!' She laughed. 'Wait, look!' She pointed to the shore where Harriet, wearing only a tank top and underwear pushed herself against a thick wave and swam. Her brown hair clung to her forehead and she refrained her teeth from chattering.

'This is crazy!' Harriet yelled.

'Yeah…' Mona stammered, paler than usual. 'Maybe we should get out.'

Harriet swiftly agreed. The sound of their laughter blended with the rhythmic crash of the waves, and Jake watched them swim back to shore, a faint smile tugging at his lips. But he remained where he was, hovering in the deep, letting the waves gently lift him. He sank onto his back, his body cradled by the water, weightless, as the cool current rocked him. It reminded him of his mother's arms. He stared at the sky, so clear and boundless above him, stretching endlessly. The cold sun beat down, bright and unforgiving, and as he closed his eyes, the light flooded through his eyelids, glowing yellow, warming his face. For a fleeting moment, he felt a deep, overwhelming sense of peace. In that stillness, it felt like he could let go completely, surrender to the calm, and simply float forever, lost in the brightness above. But it was Harriet's voice, calling his name urgently, that pierced the fragile calm. His eyelids fluttered open, and with a soft exhale, he swam back toward the shore,

The drive home was long. They got stuck in thunderous traffic. It was cold too, for the heating barely worked, but the three spoke loud and often, giggling at their adventure, forgetting the reality that loomed ahead.

That night, back at home, Harriet played the violin for Mona and Jake, the soft sound of her bow gliding across the strings filling the room with a rich, soothing melody. She played with her eyes closed, lost in the music, her body swaying gently with each note. The room seemed to disappear around them as the music took on a life of its own, weaving around them like an invisible thread binding them together.

Mona, sitting across from Jake, caught his eye and mouthed softly, *She's better than you were.*

The notes, for the first time in twenty years, made Jake's fingers itch. But he did not take the violin from his daughter and play. Instead, he watched silently, dutifully, as he had her entire life wondering how he had been so lucky to have Harriet as his daughter. It was a night that felt like it could go on forever. He wished it had. For the next day, his consultant rang and he was informed his cancer was in fact not treatable. He had only a year to live.

CHAPTER 6
TIMELESS

Jake stared at the red jelly on his table, its vivid colour a stark contrast against the sterile white of the room. It sat there untouched. He didn't know how long it had been there, but it didn't matter. Time seemed to stretch and blur in this place. The jelly, so simple and mundane. He had no desire to reach for it. Behind him, the ventilator hissed, the rhythmic sound filling the otherwise quiet room. It was a sound he had grown too accustomed to, the mechanical breath. The mask on his face felt like an extension of his nose. Jake closed his eyes. The room around him seemed to fade, the buzz of the machines growing muffled as darkness crept in.

When his eyes opened again, and the jelly was gone, leaving only a small, empty smear on the surface. But beside the door stood Harriet. She was chewing at the skin on the edge of her thumb, a nervous habit she had developed in the past few months. She looked so much older now, in ways he hadn't noticed until this moment. With deliberate effort, Jake tugged at his mask, lifting it slightly, and, with all the strength he could muster, he managed to rasp,

'Hey, you.'

Harriet didn't react immediately. She was beautiful, more

beautiful than he had ever seen her. The vibrant emerald
dress hugged her frame; the fur-black coat was elegant. Her
eyes, once bright and youthful, now shone with a silver-like
gleam, almost too piercing. Her lips, rouged and soft,
trembled ever so slightly, but it was the quiet sadness behind
her gaze that hit him hardest. She wasn't looking at him
when she spoke, her voice quiet yet firm.

'Auntie, are you sure?'

In his peripheral vision Mona was rummaging through the
cupboards around the room, opening and shutting doors,
discarding glove boxes and tissues, clearly searching for
something.

'Yes, Harriet. I'm sure.' Her voice cracked. 'Come and
help me find it. The nurse said she would leave it here.'

Harriet nodded again, her movement fluid, yet heavy with
purpose. As she moved about, Jake's focus wavered. He
glanced at the window, catching his reflection, a frail, ghostly
version of himself, mask still on. He hadn't taken it off. He
hadn't spoken at all. But then, Harriet leaned over him, her
hand warm and gentle on his own. Her touch was soft, but in
it, he felt her strength. Her voice, when it came, was like a
whisper of comfort.

'Dad, we're taking you somewhere, okay?' She spoke
softly, carefully, her words slow and deliberate. 'You're
coming with me and Mona, okay?'

Jake's only response was to nod, squeezing her hand with

all the force his frail body could muster.

'Got it!' Mona called, lifting a manual ventilator from the cupboard. She approached the bed, her face resolute, yet somehow gentle. Her smile, though faint, held a flicker of reassurance. 'Do you trust me, Jake?' Mona asked, her voice steady, unwavering.

Jake barely whispered, the words slipping out, barely audible. 'With my life.'

Harriet, wordlessly, turned off the ventilator behind them. The stillness of the room deepened as the machine hummed its final breath. Jake inhaled sharply, but the air was thick, congealed, burning as it filtered painfully through his lungs. It felt wrong, too sharp, too harsh. Mona moved swiftly, lifting the mask off his face and replacing it with the new one in her hands. The touch was delicate, practiced.

'I've got you,' she said, smiling softly as she began to pump the bag, the rhythmic motion calming in its steadiness. 'Come on, Harriet.' Mona nodded towards the door. 'Let's go.' With the click of the bed wheels, the room faded behind them, and Jake was gently pushed out of his room,

Jake had spent his entire life surrounded by cars, driving them, working on them, and even crawling beneath them. Grease was a constant companion, often smudged across his forehead, a mark of his craft. The last car he worked on was a Mini. It had been an easy job—a simple light bulb replacement—but it had felt anticlimactic. He had always imagined his final fix would be something exhilarating, like a sleek Rolls Royce, or, deep down, he had hoped to get his hands on the 1951 Vincent Black Lightning again. But he hadn't. The light bulb needed replacing, and once it was done, after his doctor told him his working days were over, he never stepped foot into a garage again. Funnily enough, Jake couldn't even remember the last time he had driven. But now, lying on Mona's lap in the back seat, her steady hands pumping the ventilator at regular intervals, he found himself mesmerised by the street lamps glistening past. The light slipped by, one moment blending seamlessly into the next, and he realised how beautiful it all was.

Mona yelled at Harriet to ease up on the brakes, her voice sharp but softened by the gentle rhythm of her fingers stroking Jake's hair. Her touch was delicate, her fingers long and soft, weaving through the strands like a quiet comfort. As the journey stretched on, the silence growing heavier, Mona began to hum, her voice a low, soothing melody in Jake's ear. It wasn't in English, Italian, perhaps? She interrupted her singing with a soft correction, telling him he was shifting the mask as he smiled. But she didn't tell him to stop. Instead, Jake leaned into her, resting his head against her abdomen as she cradled him gently, her warmth enveloping him. It was the warm tear that fell onto his cheek that made him realise Mona was crying.

'You know I love you, right?' Mona whispered, her voice

low. 'You've been my constant for the past damn forty years. And you know that I'll be hers now, right?'

In the front seat, Harriet slammed her hand against the indicator with frustration, cursing when the car ahead failed to signal. Jake barely registered the noise, the familiar rhythm of the drive made everything feel distant. 'I've got her like you had me,' Mona continued softly, her words wrapping around him like a promise. Jake didn't respond. When Mona began singing again, her voice a soft lullaby, he allowed himself to drift, the cadence of her song pulling him into a deep, peaceful sleep.

He was jolted awake as Mona struggled to lift him from the car, Harriet stepping in to take over the pumping of the ventilator, both of them working frantically to transfer him into the wheelchair. The pain surged through his body, sharp and unforgiving, his bones screaming in protest as they moved him.

'Be careful!' Mona snapped, her voice tinged with panic.

'I'm trying!' Harriet responded, her words tight with exertion.

'Try harder!' Mona shot back, frustration lacing her tone.

'Jesus!'

Jake nearly laughed at Mona's muttered curse, calling him a 'heavy bastard.' Once, he had been a solid, towering man. Now, he could feel the frailty of his own body, the loose skin and the wasted muscles. Once he was settled in the chair, Jake blinked once, twice. On the third blink, his eyes landed on the familiar, welcoming sight of the Faculty of Music at Eldenford. The building, always lit up at night, gleamed in the distance. Without a word, he pointed at it, and as if the very building had called to him, the wheels of his chair began rolling towards it, guiding him to the place that had always been home in a way no other place had ever been.

Harriet pushed the chair through the unlocked glass doors, their hinges groaning in protest against the quiet night. The sound of the wheelchair's rattling wheels echoed sharply against the polished marble floor, jarring and out of place in the stillness of the hallway. Jake winced until the noise softened into a hushed silence when they crossed onto the plush red carpets leading further inside. The faint scent of varnished wood and old music sheets lingered in the air.
As they moved deeper into the Faculty, the familiar surroundings stirred something in Jake, a quiet echo of the early days of his marriage. He had brought Annabelle here on an unofficial tour, proudly showing her around like a student sharing a secret world. Her laughter had danced off these very walls, her eyes wide, making the space feel new even to him. They'd crept into the building late one evening, giggling like children as she twirled through the corridors, pretending to be a student. Jake had shown her every room, every corner where he practiced, shared stories, and dreamed. She teased

him about his stern professors and hummed a melody of her own creation while running her fingers along the keys of a piano in one of the empty rooms.

'I'd have aced every class without even trying,' she teased, her eyes alight with mischief, ignoring the fact she was totally tone-deaf.

'Oh, I don't doubt that at all.' Jake replied. 'You'd have made me look bad.'

And there they were. The Silverwood Music Room, with its red benches and the grand piano, bathed in a soft, flickering glow. Candles lined the room, their warm light casting an orange hue that seemed to fill every corner. Beneath the woollen blanket draped over his legs, Jake shivered, the coolness of the room mingling with the warmth of the moment.

He was guided further into the centre of the room. Mona stood by his side, continuing to pump the ventilator, her movements steady, ensuring he could breathe through the heavy weight in his chest. Harriet knelt in front of him, her eyes never leaving his. The candlelight softened the sharp lines of her face, making her look both younger and wiser at once. The edges of her features glowed in the amber light.

'A little birdy told me that once upon a time there had been a great violinist who was supposed to perform here, but he abandoned his show for the birth of his daughter.' Harriet removed her coat and lowered it over her father. From the coat pocket, a scroll protruded slightly, the edges frayed and weathered. With a swift motion, she brandished it in front of him, the parchment unfurling with a quiet rustle. Jake's eyes flickered from the scroll to her face.

It was his song.

Harriet whispered. 'And do you see that, Dad?' She asked, pointing. He squinted his eyes, noticing his violin on its stand. 'Do you recognise it? It's yours.'

She gave him a kiss on the cheek, her lips lingering for a moment longer than usual. Silent tears began to roll down her face as she closed her eyes tightly, trying to hold onto the moment, unwilling to let him go. She took a deep, meaningful breath, her chest rising and falling with the weight of it and then stood up.

Jake had watched Harriet perform on countless stages throughout her life. He'd seen her tiny fingers fumble over piano keys, endured the blaring awkwardness of her brief stint with the trumpet, and finally witnessed her find her voice through the violin. But here, standing in the centre of the Silverwood Music Room, illuminated by the soft glow of candlelight, she looked ethereal. Her posture was poised, her fingers confident on the strings, yet there was a tenderness to her presence that struck him deeply. It wasn't just her talent, it was the quiet strength that seemed to radiate from her, filling the room like a melody only he could hear.

'This is for you, Dad.' She picked up the violin and put her chin to it. 'This piece was written and composed by Jake Robinson, performed by Harriet Robinson.' She smiled. 'A Timeless Symphony.'

Harriet closed her eyes and raised the bow, gently placing it on the strings. Slowly, she drew back her arm, caressing the instrument, leaning into it, becoming one with it. Jake watched her, his mind wandering to all the times he'd played, all the people who had listened to him. He thought of the years that had slipped by, trading his own performances for the quiet joy of listening – listening to Harriet as she found herself in music. And then, a smile spread across his face as he realised this song, his song, would linger within these walls forever.

As the music swelled and filled the room, there was a delicate shift. A shift so faint, neither Mona nor Harriet noticed it, but Jake did. He felt it stir gently in his chest, flutter through his skin, and settle into a profound stillness.

With quiet resolve, Jake reached out, stilling Mona's pumping hands. His touch, steady now, no longer trembling. Slowly, he removed the mask from his face. The violin's melody coursed through him, warming his bones, dissolving the ache from his body. He drew a deep breath as strength surged through his limbs, and with effortlessness he hadn't known in years, Jake stood from his wheelchair.

One tentative step followed another as he moved toward

the stage, his gaze fixed on Harriet. Her fingers danced over the strings, her playing unbroken, even as tears streamed silently down her face. She cried, but she played on, her music weaving the room together in a spellbinding embrace. And then, as Jake stepped into the glow of the candlelight, another presence emerged from its warmth. Annabelle. She stood close, her smile gentle.

'About time,' she whispered, her voice soft, not daring to disrupt the music.

'I'm sorry,' Jake replied, a flicker of humour in his tone. 'I was a little busy.'

'Yes,' Annabelle smiled, her gaze drifting to Harriet. 'You were.'

She extended her hand, palm open, inviting. 'Are you ready now?'

Jake hesitated, his eyes lingering on his daughter as her bow swept the strings, filling the room with the sound of her soul. 'How about a little longer?' he asked, his voice quiet.

Annabelle's smile softened, understanding etched in every feature. 'Okay,' she said gently. 'Only a little longer.'

ABOUT THE AUTHOR

Krystal Zammit is a dedicated English Teacher who brings her passion for writing into the classroom. With a Master's degree in Creative Writing from Lancaster University, Krystal leads the creative writing club at her school, nurturing the next generation of storytellers. Outside of the classroom, Krystal finds inspiration and joy in spending time with her family and friends, who continually support and encourage her creative pursuits.

TIMELESS SYMPHONY

Printed in Dunstable, United Kingdom